The Stories We Tell

Also by Devdutt Pattanaik

Pilgrim Nation

Marriage: 100 Stories Around India's Favourite Ritual

Business Sutra Series

My Gita

My Hanuman Chalisa

Ramayana Versus Mahabharata: My Playful Comparison

How to Become Rich: 12 Lessons I Learnt from Vedic and Puranic Stories

The Stories We Tell

MYTHOLOGY TO MAKE SENSE OF MODERN LIVES

....

DEVDUTT PATTANAIK

ALEPH

ALEPH

Published by
ALEPH BOOK COMPANY
An independent publishing firm
promoted by *Rupa Publications India*

First published in India in 2022
by Aleph Book Company
7/16 Ansari Road, Daryaganj
New Delhi 110 002

ISBN: 978-93-91047-82-5

3 5 7 9 10 8 6 4

Typeset in Garamond Premier Pro by
Special Effects Graphics Design Co, Mumbai
Printed at Parksons Graphics Pvt. Ltd. Mumbai

Dedicated to all those who recognize stories as the containers of wisdom.

Contents

Author's Note

The Stories We Tell has its origins in a webcast that I initiated in 2020 from 21 March to 31 May, during the early days of India's countrywide lockdown to combat Covid-19. People were terrified of the virus and I wanted to lift their spirits by telling them stories from our mythology that would make them less anxious. As these stories were told from 4 p.m. to 5 p.m. around teatime, I named my webcast **Teatime Tales**. I genuinely believed the lockdown would end in a few weeks, but it then became clear that we would remain indoors for a long time. I knew I would not be able to sustain the enterprise endlessly. So, I decided to end it gracefully after seventy-two episodes. Why seventy-two? Well, you will find out in the book. All seventy-two episodes from the original webcast have been archived on my YouTube channel, DevduttMyth.

The Stories We Tell extends and deepens the stories and interpretations of stories and myths that appeared on Teatime Tales. I am thankful to Prathyush Parashuraman for helping summarize each episode and putting these stories together.

Devdutt Pattanaik
Mumbai
October 2021

Introduction: How Mythology Makes Sense of Modern Lives

Fact is everybody's truth.
Fiction is nobody's truth.
Myth is somebody's truth.

Myth is how people imagine the world.

Myths are usually embedded in sacred stories, and so we look to these sacred stories to stitch together a narrative of how many of our ancestors thought—from the mantras in the Vedic tradition, to the bardic suta parampara, as seen in the Ramayana, Mahabharata, and Puranas; and the Jataka and Jain tales. In this book, we will also go further afield—to Arabian, Greek, Roman, Egyptian, and Norse myths—and even explore how myths from the Islamic and Christian worlds changed on Indian soil, just as myths from Buddhism changed in China and elsewhere. What you will realize is that some feelings are felt everywhere.

The story, the katha, is the building block of mythology. Its telling is meant to entertain, educate, and once over, be meditated upon. It helps you indulge in an alternate world with characters who teach you people before us have imagined the same world we live in. I hope this book, with its bite-sized chapters, which can be consumed over tea, or coffee, does just that.

Throughout this book, and through its stories, I will attempt to do two things.

First, use the Puranic framework of desha–kala–guna i.e., geography–history–attributes to discuss various topics in mythology. This is to remind you that all stories exist in a context. The ideas may be timeless but the stories are not. Stories change over time, over space, and with people who transmit them.

Secondly, use a 'post-structuralist' framework to think about myths. This simply means I don't care much for watertight categories and strict labels. I think they are helpful in trying to organize the complexity of our history, but I also know that these categories are created by people with their own biases, agendas, and levels of knowledge. Most certainly people in the 'Dark Ages' did not think that they were living through the Dark Ages. Mohenjo-daro and Harappa are all contemporary names. No one knows what these cultures called themselves, though we know that Mesopotamians referred to people of the Indus Valley Civilization, or at least its coast, as Meluhha. Thus, labels and structures, while helpful, are also limiting.

Before we begin, I must note some fairly obvious things. But I think writing them down explicitly has merit. It will help you engage with the stories better.

First, mythology is *not* history. Its purpose is different. History is a record of the past. Mythology explains how cultures imagine the world, and their past. It is true that some historical characters, over time, have been mythologized. Like Siddhartha Gautama, about whose life Asvaghosha wrote, but only 500 years after the Buddha's death. Similarly, with the Gospels on Jesus Christ and the Hadith on Prophet Muhammad and the Digvijaya of Adi Shankaracharya—their life stories were written centuries after they passed away and have been embellished with metaphors and fantastic symbols to reinforce a particular worldview or their status as a religious leader. These stories were never meant to be historical records. The idea was more important than the fact.

Mythology is not parable either. Parables are prescriptive, while mythology is structural, about origins and organization of nature and culture, in which parables may be located. Mythology may be spiritual, which is nothing but deep psychology, expressed in supernatural language. Mythology informs religion, which uses the supernatural to get people to act in a particular way.

About history itself, we didn't have the concept of it until 200 years ago. It was only in the nineteenth century that scholars decided to look back and see if there were evidence-based statements we could make about our past. We began to call that activity 'history'. Stories without evidence but of value politically became legends. They were key to legitimize certain claims. And stories beyond science, dealing with the supernatural, soul, God, and afterlife became myth. Myths, like I mentioned in the beginning, are subjective truths. You *can* believe God exists and created the universe or that there is justice in the world. But that doesn't mean it's a measurable evidence-based fact. By the way, money is not objective truth; it works because we believe in it, making money a myth too, one that even atheist secular scientists believe in. Ultimately, we are trying to make sense of our lives, to make sense of the horror of living. Science tells you how the world came into being but only myth can tell you why the world came into being. Myths help us navigate our way.

Secondly, I am not a lawyer, so do not expect me to defend any stories or justify any action of a god or a hero. I am not interested in 'the truth'. I am interested in the collective imagination of people, and I enjoy comparing shifts in these cultural imaginations over history and geography.

Broadly speaking, there are four paths to knowledge as per Indian epistemology (theory of knowledge):

1. Anubhav or experience.
2. Anuman or inference.
3. Shabda or testimony.
4. Upaman or measurement and comparison.

In this book and, generally, most of my books, I use the fourth path.

The Tantric Saraswati symbol

In my study, I have a Tantric Saraswati symbol on the wall behind me (you can see it on the cover of the book). I was often asked by people who joined in during the talks about what it represents. It is a pattern that begins with one seed and slowly sprouts towards infinity. That is exactly like the life cycle of a story—every story is a little seed, you tell that story, and from that story, ideas emerge. 1 becomes 3 becomes 5 becomes 7 becomes 9...the numbers keep increasing. Or, alternatively, it could be seen as the reverse as infinity becoming finite over time. The image is, thus, one and infinity simultaneously, depending on whether we see it from bottom to top, or from top to bottom. Just like the image I had in the background of my videos, let's keep this idea in the background of our thoughts as we read—to be cognizant of the infinite as a goal, and the finite as a way to make sense and grapple with it.

Remember what I always say:

Within infinite myths lies an eternal truth
Who sees it all?
Varuna has but a thousand eyes
Indra, a hundred
You and I, only two.

The Stories

Tale 1

....

Remembering Stories

I divide all the stories I hear, first, historically, then geographically.

Historically, I use the 500-year model, where I divide the last 4,000 years into 500-year intervals—this is a broad brushstroke, but it's helpful in categorizing.

1. Before 2000 BCE: Pre-history ending with the Indus Valley Civilization. The seals of these silent cities tell many stories that await decoding.

2. 2000 BCE–1500 BCE: Little is known of this period in history.

3. 1500 BCE–1000 BCE: The Vedic period when the four Vedas were compiled and we learn of Kurus and Bharatas for the first time in the Punjab–Haryana region. We have a few stories where Indra is the hero.

4. 1000 BCE–500 BCE: The Upanishads were composed and rebirth as an idea became firmly established in the Gangetic plains.

5. 500 BCE–0: Buddhism and Jainism come to the fore with Ashoka and Kharavela. The Ramayana and Mahabharata are being written. The Jatakas

are not only being written but also carved on the railings of stupas. Shatavahanas rule in the Deccan.

6. 0–500 CE: This is when the Kushanas, with roots in Southwestern China, come to India having conquered vast parts of Central Asia and Afghanistan. Images of Surya begin to be seen. This is also when the Guptas are powerful, their gold coins a sign of prosperity, and the image of gods with many hands becomes popularized. The first images of Vishnu as Varaha are found in Madhya Pradesh around this time. Tamil Sangam literature emerges with stories that show the domination of Buddhist and Jain ideas in the South, before gradually giving way to stories of Shiva and Vishnu.

7. 500 CE–1000 CE: The Puranas are formally written down. Images of Vishnu in Ananta Shayana, where he is sleeping peacefully on the serpent Ananta, are seen for the first time in Deogarh near Jhansi in one of the earliest free-standing Hindu temples. Southern India becomes a major force. This is also the period of decline in Buddhism.

8. 1000 CE–1500 CE: Mahmud of Ghazni attacks India, followed by Ghuri who migrates to India to create the Delhi Sultanate. Some of the biggest temples like the Madurai Meenakshi and the Jagannath Puri were built during this period. This is when the Vijayanagara kings rose in the Deccan

and defended 'Hindu dharma' from what they called 'Turuku dharma'. This is also when the first regional works on the Ramayana and Mahabharata appear in southern and eastern India.

9. 1500–2000 CE: This is when Sikhism emerges and the Bhakti movement, which comes from the South, becomes very strong in the North. The Mughals, Marathas, British Raj all shared power and prestige during this period, until India became a republic in 1947. This is the time when Rajput epics are composed in the North and almost every region of India has its own regional body of stories.

Geographically, most of the stories with Hindu roots that we know, such as the Ramayana and Mahabharata, are from North India but they transform as they spread to other parts of the subcontinent. Though Bhakti literature emerges around the eighth century CE from the South, it seeps into the North where it bears fruit around the fifteenth century CE.

So, how does this framework help? The moment someone says Ramanuja I think Tamil Nadu, I think twelfth century CE. The moment someone says Alvar I think Tamil Nadu, I think around the sixth–seventh century CE. History and geography categorizes the stories, figures, and myths, like different shelves in a cabinet. Sometimes the first thing I think of is the place of the story, desha. Sometimes the first thing I think of is the time of the story, kala. Sometimes the first thing I think of is the theme or attribute of the story, guna. Thus, the desha–kala–guna framework helps.

I find geography is important because local stories have *always* been more important than the Sanskrit ones, because Sanskrit was *never* the language of the masses. In Maharashtra, where I live, it is the local Marathi songs such as Abhangs and Ovis, and local Marathi figures like Eknath, Jnaneshwar, Khandoba, Pandharpur, Vitthal Swami that are of greater importance. In Odisha, where my parents were from, most of the stories are about Jagannath and Sakshi Gopal. In Andhra Pradesh, the stories are about Annamayya and Tirupati.

It is also important to note that in fixating on the big picture, the Hindu–Buddhist–Jain story structures, we forget how these stories percolate into local traditions, or how local traditions affect those bigger narratives we today consider 'mainstream'. We overlook Sikh narratives that emerged in the last 500 years, or myths that came into India from Persia and Central Asia, via Zoroastrianism and Islam. Additionally, India has more than 500 tribes comprising over 8 per cent of India's population, and each tribe has its own unique stories. Many tribes like those in Jharkhand mainly follow a distinct animistic religion— Sarnaism. Many others have converted to Christianity. What stories do they tell one another?

Tale 2

History and Mythology

It is important to map mythology onto history, but never confuse one for the other.

Let's look at the story in the Ramayana, where Shabari is feeding Rama berries that she has bitten. This was not a story in Valmiki's or Tulsidas's Ramayana. This comes only around the eighteenth century, in the Hindi version of the text. There is also a story of Rama asking a Savaruni, a tribal woman, in the forest for a mango that has been bitten into because its sweetness is known. This story is found in Odisha around 500 years ago. This is Shabari's protoform. So, using the history and geography of stories, we can attempt to track where these stories came from, and if we are lucky, why these stories were told in the first place.

Similarly, the idea of Vishnu being an avatara is not found in the Mahabharata or Ramayana. It is only around 500 CE, in the Puranas, that we see this. Even the word we often use today—dharma—is scarcely used in the Rig Veda and not given importance in the Upanishads. It is only in the Mahabharata and Ramayana that this idea explodes. Why? We have to search for reasons, and this is why placing mythological texts in their historical context is important—to find answers to such questions.

Bhakti Kavya became important from 1600 CE. The

emotional thrust comes from the Alvars and Nayanars in 600 CE in Tamil Nadu, from where Vallabhacharya and Ramananda take it to the North, where Kabir, Mirabai, Nars, Haridas, Jagannath Das, and Raskhan take this idea further.

Why is the time period important here?

Because there is a strong correlation between the arrival of Islam and Bhakti. Both influence each other. Nirguna Bhakti, that worships a formless god like Allah, becomes very important over time. Similarly, the use of flowers becomes important in the Sufi 'dargah' tradition in India. Over time, we see numerous cultural exchanges, and through this the stories change, and their meaning, too, changes.

For example, Sikhism comes at the intersection of Hinduism and Islam. Founded by Guru Nanak over five centuries ago, it initially came out of the Bhakti tradition of Hinduism, and then slowly crystallized into its own religion, rejecting the caste system and idolatry entirely. A book is given a lot of importance here—this is an Islamic influence, from their reverence for the Holy Quran. But the book is placed on an asan, with a chadar, on a palki, under an umbrella—this spectacle is a Hindu idea.

Thus, even the geography of Sikhism makes sense—in the Northwest, where Islam and Hinduism meet. Before, Sikhism was seen as a part of Hinduism and Sufism, but in the twentieth century there was a movement to consider it a separate religion; it became formalized.

Sikhism over time also developed its own unique

traditions, the main theme being social equality. Langar, the community kitchen, was a very important element. All the poems by saints were compiled and collected in the Guru Granth Sahib, found in every gurdwara. This goes to show that, if you want, every aspect of our life can be seen as a product of the churn of culture over time.

The Act of Seeing

Words have form, meaning has no form. But if there are no words, how does one communicate meaning? Words are thus a vessel through which meaning is transmitted. So if you don't see the form, the sagun, how can you grasp the formless, the nirgun? The ability to look at the meaning beyond the form is what we mean when we say darshan.

In Durga Puja, the most important ritual is Chokkhu Daan, where you give eyes to the deity. The statue of Durga Puja has no value until the ritual, and after that moment it stops being a statue but becomes a living, breathing entity.

The act of seeing and being seen is so important. Duryodhana spent his entire life not being seen. His father, Dhritarashtra, was blind, not able to see, and his mother, Gandhari, blindfolded herself, not willing to see. What do you expect such a child to become when he grows up?

On the other hand, you have Krishna. He has two fathers who adore him—Vasudeva and Nanda—and two mothers—Yashoda and Devaki. He is surrounded by love, and so when he sees Duryodhana, he sees a poor man. How do you deal with someone who has never been seen?

Darshan is not about seeing the visible body; it is about seeing the invisible potential. Look at Jagannath of Puri—a statue with no hands, no legs, no ears, and no eyelids and yet he is supposed to represent perfection! How? It is only because while the form is imperfect, the idea it communicates remains perfection! And when we do a darshan of him, we must tap into that formless perfection, and not be stuck in the form. Likewise, in Duryodhana, there exists the potential to be perfect, if he is willing to outgrow his insecurities, his parents notwithstanding.

Tale 4

....

Three Steps of Vamana

In the Puranas, we find the story of King Mahabali who was generous to a fault because he would give anything that was asked of him. The gods could not defeat him for he made everyone happy. Vishnu, then takes the form of a dwarf, Vamana, and asks Mahabali for three paces of land. When granted, Vamana becomes big, and with two paces traverses all three worlds. Now Vamana asks, 'How do I get the third pace that I have been promised?' Mahabali, at a loss for words and actions, finally places Vamana's feet on his head—and is thus pushed under the earth.

The popular version of this story shows Bali as arrogant, Vishnu as good, and the story thus becomes about the vanquishing of the bad by the good through trickery. There is also a Marxist version of this story where the king is representative of a land of radical equality and Vishnu is the evil Brahmin who rattles this universe.

But is there more to the story? There's a small detail regarding Shukracharya, Mahabali's guru, that is often forgotten. He is suspicious of this dwarf and asks Mahabali to reconsider giving him the three paces of land, but the king does not pay attention to his guru's doubts. For the deed by which Vamana will be granted three paces of land, Mahabali has to pour water over land from the kamandalu, the water pot with a spout. To prevent this from happening, Shukracharya becomes a flower and clogs the spout of the kamandalu to stop the water from flowing out. Vamana, smart as he is, takes a blade of grass to unclog it, pressing it into the spout, at which point Shukracharya becomes human, howling, as his eye is pierced; he loses an eye!

Shukracharya is also known as Bhrigu, associated with the asuras who live below the earth where all the wealth, all the Lakshmi, is. This is why Lakshmi is called Pataal Nivasini, resident of subterranean regions; she is also called Poulomi, the daughter of Puloman, the king of the asuras; and Bhargavi, the daughter of Bhrigu.

If you think about it, you realize that all the wealth underground—gold, coal, lapis lazuli—has no value unless it is pulled up above the ground. Now imagine if you could keep extracting value from the underworld— what would happen? That is exactly what Mahabali, the asura, is doing. He is giving people whatever they want, whenever they want. This is what Vishnu wants to put an end to, for he understands that while wants may be infinite, resources are finite. This is what Vamana is trying to communicate in his Trivikrama form, that human ambition can *never* be satisfied entirely. No king can satisfy the needs of his people forever, for needs very easily turn into greed. Generosity does not work unless balanced with contentment.

....

Appropriation or Exchange

I have been hearing this statement for a while now, about the cultural appropriation of yoga, and how only Indians should teach yoga because it is an Indian concept. First of all, this language of cultural appropriation is nurtured, popularized, and deployed by the West; it is alien to India. Who decides what idea is stolen and what idea is exchanged? Yoga was brought to America by Indians, which is very different from Africans who were dragged from Africa to work as slaves in America. Yoga reached America voluntarily.

Yes, there is a capitalist side to it, with the yoga industry reducing, in its most egregious form, the Buddha to a spa icon. In nature, the big fish eat the small fish. This is why Manu decided to save the small fish and put the fish in his kamandalu to protect it from the jungle law. This counter-force is dharma. Yes, the tendency of people is to steal and appropriate. But civilization turns raiding into trading, appropriation into exchange. Building walls does not create civilization.

Hinduism is based on plurality, and the New World is based on equality. There is a fundamental dissonance between these two concepts. Plurality appreciates the dynamic between the strong and the weak, how natural tendency is for the strong to consume the weak, and how dharma seeks to counter this natural tendency. But in the West, activists tend to see the strong as the enemy and we are told the meek will inherit heaven while the strong have to repent for their sins. The language of dharma should be distinguished from the language of equality.

There is a very sweet story of the squirrel in the Ramayana. When people were carrying big boulders from the Himalayas to make the Ram Setu, a squirrel would make itself wet and roll in the sand and pour that sand over the bridge. Everyone makes fun of him, but Rama thanks him, 'Look at it from his perspective. He is giving 100 per cent, and you are giving 100 per cent, so what's the difference?' This is a great example where equality is rejected. Everyone cannot carry the same weight, but everyone must carry the weight they are able to carry. The West universalizes all ideas. Dharma prefers to contextualize. The West loves to judge as God is a judge in Western religions like Christianity and Islam. In dharma, God empathizes with human frailties and nudges us to do better. Hence, the avataras.

I once received a WhatsApp forward about the Dashavatara, the ten avataras of Vishnu being mapped onto Darwin's evolution theory—from a fish, to an amphibian, to an animal, to a half human–half animal to a fully formed human. This I found not just funny but also a bit dangerous, because it creates a hierarchy among the avataras, which was never the intention. Vishnu, the turtle, is not more or less evolved than Vishnu, the fish. Both are revealing the concept of dharma through ideas like compassion and collaboration.

If we look at the human avataras—from Vamana, a Brahmin, we come to Parashurama, a half-Brahmin, half-Kshatriya, to Rama who is a Kshatriya, to Krishna whose caste is ambiguous because he is a gwala (cowherd) and a sarathi (charioteer). Then comes the Buddha, who renounces caste, and then Kalkin, an outsider who comes to your universe to destroy it. Is that evolution? Or something else is being communicated here?

It should be noted here that Kalkin is not the destroyer of evil; 'evil' is a Christian concept. St John's Book of Revelation describes a fight between Jesus and the Devil in Armageddon, a confrontation. In Islam, too, there is the idea of the Mahdi and Isa, the prophets of God, banding together to fight Iblis and Dajjal, the forces of evil. Kalkin, however, is not a messiah.

....

Ghosts as Storytellers

King Vikramaditya was challenged by a Tantric guru to capture a Vetal, an Indian ghost This meant that he had to go to a banyan tree in a cemetery, where, like the roots which dangle, Vetals would be hanging. In the middle of the night, when Vikramaditya reached the cemetery, he saw these figures who didn't have flesh on their bodies. They were slippery and so it was hard to hold onto them. Vetals are dead but have not crossed over to the land of the dead. They remain on earth as ghosts, struggling without a body.

When Vikramaditya succeeded in capturing a Vetal, he remembered being warned that if he spoke a single word, the Vetal would be free to run away. The Vetal was desperate to make Vikramaditya speak so he could be freed. Knowing that Vikramaditya had a huge ego, the Vetal pretended not to believe that he was the real Vikramaditya. So, he began to tell him engaging stories and parables and asked questions to prove himself as truly Vikramaditya. So, whenever Vikramaditya, in his ego to prove himself right, slipped up and gave the answer, the Vetal would be free to run away.

This kept going on, and Vikramaditya kept forgetting his mission, absorbed in the story that the Vetal was telling him, and answering the questions because he had the answer. The moment he opened his mouth, the Vetal escaped. This went on and on, every night. Vikramaditya would capture the Vetal, only to be tricked by its enchanting story into forgetting his mission.

This happened twenty-four times. Then the Vetal asked the one question which even Vikramaditya could not answer: how will you die?

With this ends the Vetala Pachisi, the twenty-five stories of the Vetal.

Later, when the Vetal became his friend, Vikramaditya asked him the same question that he was unable to answer: how was he going to die? The Vetal said, 'You will be killed by a potter's son who loves to play on the shali tree!'

Vikramaditya then goes in search of that son, Shalivahana, wondering how he is going to kill him. He notices that Shalivahana is making clay toys, pretending to be the king of them all.

Shalivahana would throw these dolls into a well, and the nagas who lived in this well, blessing the waters, gave the dolls magic powers to be able to rise back to life. Every night they would come and whisper to Shalivahana that they would support him when he replaced Vikramaditya as king.

As fate would have it, these dolls came to life and fought Vikramaditya, defeating him eventually. The dolls or bommais that are exhibited in the South Indian golu during Navratri are supposed to be in memory of Shalivahana who was supposed to be a king in the

Deccan region, in the South, while Vikramaditya ruled in the North.

But the story doesn't end here.

Since Shalivahana was from a potter's family, he did not know how to speak Sanskrit. His wife worried about how he would become a king if he did not know the language. So, he called his ministers to teach him Sanskrit. Gunadhya, one of his ministers, told it would take him fifteen years to learn Sanskrit. But fifteen years was too long!

Then, another minister promised that it would take fifteen days, that there was a simple method of learning Sanskrit and its rules of grammar. He was Panini, the person who wrote the first book of grammar. He taught Shalivahana how to speak, with grammatical rules in place, for the first time.

Gunadhya took a vow to stop speaking Sanskrit if Shalivahana learned it in fifteen days. Needless to say, Panini succeeded and Gunadhya stopped speaking the language and went into the forest.

After many years, Gunadhya's students from the forest come to the king, who now only reads, writes, and speaks in Sanskrit. The students have a book that captures all the stories of the world. Shalivahana takes the book from them but cannot understand it because it is in Pisachi bhasha, the language of the forest dwellers, and the king only knows Sanskrit, and is uninterested in anything non-Sanskrit.

The story goes that Shiva was narrating the Ocean of

Stories, *Katha Sarit Sagar,* to his wife, Shakti. The stories were overheard by Shiva's attendants, the ganas, who passed it on to the ghosts, the pisachas. They were, in turn, overheard and understood by Gunadhya, who had sworn never to speak in Sanskrit and Prakrit, having lost the bet to his king. Gunadhya wrote the stories down using his blood as ink and gave it to King Shalivahana. But the king found the language strange and felt Gunadhya was simply a madman who claimed to speak the 'language of ghosts', Pisachi bhasha. So, Gunadhya, with a heavy heart, began reading the stories aloud in the forest to the birds and the beasts; burning the manuscript page by page as he did so. The king, who had rejected the manuscript, happened to be in the forest hunting, and observed the birds and beasts listening spellbound to the strange language of the sage. He realized that Gunadhya was not a madman as he first suspected, but was, in fact, truly telling a story known only to ghosts until then. He stopped Gunadhya and saved what remained of the book. Of the seven sections of the great narrative, only one remained from which all the fantastic adventure stories of the world have come into being. These stories have no religious leanings but were eventually absorbed and turned into Buddhist, Jain, and Hindu stories.

In life, you need to learn many languages to be successful. The king who was a potter's son learned Sanskrit. The minister who knows Sanskrit, renounces it, and learns Pisachi. With Prakrit he communicated with the potters, with Sanskrit he communicated with the courtly ministers, and with Pisachi he communicated with the birds and animals of the forest. The moral here is simple: the more stories you want to know, the more languages you must learn. (Or, the more translations you must read!)

Tale 7

....

Puzzles for the King

Each of the twenty-five stories that the Vetal told Vikramaditya deal with puzzles that need to be resolved. Let me tell you some of these stories.

Once, there were three men who were deeply in love with the same girl. Through a tragic set of circumstances, the girl dies of an illness. In grief, one of the lovers jumps onto her funeral pyre, his flesh melting with hers. Another lover refuses to leave the crematorium. The third lover learns magic and sorcery to bring her back to life. Lo and behold, he succeeds in bringing her back to flesh and blood, but along with her, even the lover who threw himself into the fire is brought back to life.

Now, the Vetal asks Vikramaditya, 'This girl is standing with her three lovers. If you are truly Vikramaditya, tell me which of the three men she will choose to marry.'

Vikramaditya, after thinking a bit, says, 'She will marry the man who stayed in the crematorium. This is because the man who brought her back to life has now become like her father, and the one she came back to life with, becomes like her brother. Therefore, it is the one who remained in the crematorium whom she must marry!'

Here's another Vikram–Vetal parable to give you a

flavour of the kind of tales that were spun.

Once, there was a king who had three queens. One of the queens would get bruised whenever a lotus petal fell on her body. The second queen would get burned when moonlight fell on her. And the third queen would bruise and bleed when the sound of a hammer was heard. The Vetal asks Vikramaditya, 'Which of the three queens is the most delicate?'

Vikramaditya replies, 'It must be the queen who is bruised by the sound of a hammer! Because in both the lotus-bruising and moon-burn, there is physical contact between the object causing the bruises and the queen— either by the petal or the flash of light that touches the skin. The third queen is bruised without any physical contact and thus must be the most delicate!'

These stories were written somewhere between the fifth and tenth centuries CE in India, in the post-Gupta, pre-Rajput era.

Tale 8
....

Sulaiman the Wise

Sulaiman or Solomon (famous in Islam, Christianity, and Judaism), the great king of Jerusalem built the First Temple to Jehovah using stone. His subjects, who used to live in woollen tents, were enthralled. There were whispers about a worm, Shamir, that Sulaiman had got from paradise, that could slice rocks into bricks. The jinns, who were Sulaiman's slaves, would build the temple while he would watch them from his throne, his takht, holding his staff.

Once, there was a man who had three sons. When the man died, the three sons fought over his property. One of the sons had two heads, so when the three brothers entered Sulaiman's court, he saw four heads. The one with two heads said, 'I have two heads, so I deserve two shares of the property.'

Sulaiman comes up with a very nice judgement, 'Yes, there might be four heads, four mouths, but there are only three stomachs, so I will divide the property into three parts, each one getting one part.'

This sounds like a Vikram–Vetal story! Vikramaditya's throne was in fact very similar to Sulaiman's takht that had lion and tiger statues that would come alive if anyone who wasn't Sulaiman tried to sit on the throne. This is cultural diffusion.

Sulaiman of the Perso–Arabic tradition is a reflection of Solomon from the Bible. In the Bible, two mothers come to Solomon with a child, each mother saying that the child is hers. Solomon says, 'In that case, divide the child into two, one part for each mother.' One of the mothers is happy with this, while the other refuses in alarm, telling the other mother to keep the child. Noticing this, Solomon then says, 'This child must belong to the mother who wants the child to remain alive even if it means parting from it, and not the woman who is happy to see it killed!'

Tale 9

Did Ravana Understand the Veda?

When Sita is kidnapped, Rama has only one piece of information—that she has been taken south. So, he heads south where he meets Hanuman, a monkey or vanar (vana-nara: man in a forest), in the form of a Brahmin who speaks pure Sanskrit. Lakshmana is very suspicious, but Rama allays his suspicions saying, 'Let's first talk to him.' Which means, when you see something different, while our natural reaction is to be feared or fearful, we mustn't be suspicious before we have even engaged.

Rama speaks to the vanar as an equal. When Ravana speaks to Hanuman, he also speaks in Sanskrit. However, while Rama is impressed and replies in Sanskrit, Ravana is mad, because it is important to him to be the only person able to speak Sanskrit; instead of curiosity, he is insecure. A lot of people say that Ravana is a Shiv bhakt, and knows the Vedas. But knowing does not mean one has atma-gyana, for where there is realization of atma, there cannot be insecurity. When Hanuman asks Ravana to give him a place to sit, Ravana does not give him one, and so Hanuman coils his tail to make himself a seat.

You can notice here what Valmiki is trying to say. That knowledge doesn't make you a good person. Ravana, despite being so well read and entrenched in the Vedic traditions, turns to violence, greed, and insecurity easily.

The same can be said about wealth and power, where despite Ravana's Pushpa vahana, and Chandrahas sword, he is still arrogant. There is a difference between what you have and what you are. You can have knowledge, material wealth, and power. But strip them off and you realize who you really are.

When the arrow fells Ravana at the end of the war, and he is on the ground dying, Rama tells Lakshmana to go to him, and learn from him, for he is learned, even if he is arrogant. Ravana doesn't give Lakshmana any of his knowledge, turning the other way, and Lakshmana angered goes back to Rama. Rama then asks, 'Were you standing by his feet or by his head?' Lakshmana says he was standing by Ravana's head, since they had vanquished him. Rama said, 'I am not telling you to claim knowledge from him as a victor, but to learn from him as a student. He's insecure, so sit by his feet.' Ravana, realizing how transparent he is to Rama, then teaches Lakshmana everything he knows.

Tale 10

The Jain Mahabharata

The Mahabharata is the story of Pandavas fighting Kauravas. But the Jain Mahabharata or Harivamsa is different. It is a battle between Krishna in Mathura on one side, and Jarasandha, the emperor of Magadha, on the other side. They fight because Jarasandha is trying to establish and expand his empire. Krishna disapproves of this, and there is tension brewing between them.

Another reason for this war is that Jarasandha married off his two daughters to Kansa. So, when Krishna kills Kansa, Jarasandha retaliates by attacking and burning Mathura as revenge for his daughters' widowhood. Krishna ends up leaving Mathura, going west to Dwarka as a refugee.

Krishna is from the West of India, and Jarasandha is from the East. In the Ramayana we have Ayodhya in the North and Lanka in the South. The two great Indian epics cover the length and breadth of India.

Krishna, married to Rukmini, has a son with her, named Pradyumna. When he is born, a rakshasa, Sambhara, picks him up and throws him into the river, where a fish swallows him; a fisherman who catches the fish, finds the child. He gives the child to a woman yearning for one, and that woman happens to be the wife of Sambhara—Mayawati.

The child, however, instantly turns into a handsome

young man and now Mayawati wants to marry him. But Pradyumna resists this idea, telling her that she's his mother. It is at that moment that a voice from the heavens booms, and tells them about who they were in their previous birth—the mother was Rati Devi and Pradyumna was Kama Deva. Shiva had opened his third eye turning Kama Deva to ashes, and Rati Devi was told that in the next birth they would unite, as Pradyumna and Mayawati. So, this becomes a story of Mayawati marrying the child she saves. This story comes from the Bhagavata Purana.

In the Jain narrative, however, when Pradyumna tells Mayawati—here, Kanchanmala—that they cannot marry, she gets mad, and goes to her husband and tells him that this young man misbehaved with her. But the husband doesn't believe her because Pradyumna is like her son, and so he wouldn't dare misbehave with her in this manner. She then goes to her other sons, and tells them to torture him, and they acquiesce to their mother's demand. Sometimes, they throw him into a well, and at other times, throw him into a fire, but Pradyumna always returns unscathed. So, in the Jain tradition, this story becomes not one of reunion, but of Pradyumna's adventures, and of how he survives his stepbrothers' plots to kill him. Jains venerate Krishna's cousin Neminatha, as a Jina, conqueror of the mind. Neminatha's symbol is a conch shell reminding us of Krishna's conchshell, the Panchajanya.

Tale 11

....

Kartikeya

Kartikeya, the son of Shiva and Parvati/Shakti, the Lord of Tuesday, associated with Mars and wars, is also known as Murugan, Skanda, Shanmukha, or Saravana, in the South.

While Ganesha, his brother, is associated with literary activities, Kartikeya, with a spear in his hand, is young, virile, and beautiful, associated, not just with violence and war, but also prosperity. His symbol is that of a rooster, who fights aggressively, maintaining a pecking order. In Pehowa, near Kurukshetra, there is a village with a temple where women are not allowed. The men here pour oil over Kartikeya's idol. It is said that after the Mahabharata war, Yudhishthira, guilt-ridden, did penance here by pouring oil over Kartikeya. Kartikeya is here visualized as a skeletal god—his body comprises just bones. This is because of the Tantric idea that your bones and nerves come from your father, while your flesh and blood are from your mother. A temple tale informs us that when Kartikeya storms out of his house in a rage after an altercation, his mother tells him to return everything that is hers, and so he gives her back the flesh.

One of the main and earliest sources of Kartikeya is in Sangam poetry that refers to him as the 'red god'. The story of him being Shiva's son comes from the

Mahabharata. Idols of him as Kumara can be dated back to the Gupta period—here, he is associated with the peacock and the rooster. Curiously, it is from the Gupta period that he stopped being worshipped individually in the North.

There is a sweet story to explain this relative absence in the North today. When Ardhanareshwara—half Shiva, half Parvati—manifests before him, he asks, 'What happened to the other half of my mother and father?' Ardhanareshwara tells him that the other half of Shiva became all the men in the world, and the other half of Shakti became all the women in the world. So Kartikeya now cannot fight men, nor can he marry women. He thus heads South. Shakti, dejected but caring, tells Hidimba to take all the Himalayan mountains southwards so Kartikeya doesn't miss home. That is why mountains in South India are often called Dakshin Kailash.

In the North, he is thus considered a brahmachari, while in the South he has two wives, Valli (a tribal maiden) and Sena (Indra's daughter). These two marriages also work as a metaphor—that God is connected to both the earth and the sky. Curiously, Ganesha is considered married in the North, while he is a brahmachari in the South.

While the popularly told story pegs him as the son of Shiva and Shakti, one of the stories relates Kartikeya to Agni. The story goes that Agni was infatuated by the seven wives of the Saptarishis, and decides to pursue an affair with each of them. Agni's wife, Swaha, told him that they were married to rishis who might curse him in anger if he had an affair with them. Every day, Swaha, without Agni knowing, would take the form of one of the rishis' wives, and have an intimate encounter with Agni. After this happens six times, a child is born, and is called Murugan or Kartikeya. Imagine, to conceive this great god of war, Agni had to consummate the relationship six times! So Kartikeya is masculine to the power of six. Shiva does not feature in this story.

When the rishis find out about his birth, six of them reject their wives thinking they had sexual relations with Agni. The six wives leave home in anger, going eastwards, and become the Krittikas, or the Pleiades constellation. All six women decided to wreak vengeance on this child because of whom they were thrown out, but when he looks at them and says, 'Mother, you've come, I'll be Kartikeya (from Krittika) from today onwards!', all their anger melts away.

The most popular story regarding Kartikeya, comes from the Shiva Purana. Here, he kills Tarakasura, an asura who could only be killed by a six-day-old baby. But which six-day-old baby could defeat this ruthless powerful asura? When Tarakasura causes havoc, Brahma advises the gods to search for a man whose semen is so potent with inner fire that the child born from it would vanquish this asura. Naturally, the gods go to Shiva. Since the seed should not be cooled by the feminine womb, they collect the seed, but it's so hot that Agni, Vayu, and even Ganga could not cool it. When it falls on the reeds on the banks of the Ganga, the forests catch fire because of it. From that fire, Kartikeya, with six heads, is born.

So, if someone asks, who is Kartikeya's mother, who does one name? Parvati? Swaha? Shiva? Vayu? Ganga? Krittikas? And is his father Shiva or Agni? Is he married or unmarried? There are so many variations, reminding us of India's diversity and the complex layers of history.

Fish

Jhulelal, the revered deity of the Sindhis, is represented as a man with a thick white beard. He is sitting on a lotus, surrounded by the silver palla fish. The palla fish is unique, in that it is born at the source of a river, and after spending its life flowing with it, goes against the current, back to the source of the river, to lay its eggs. Jains believe that when tirthankaras are born, their mothers have a special dream with idols of gods, jewels, and a pair of fish swimming in opposite directions, all of which are considered auspicious.

In the Islamic tradition, too, there is the story of Al-Khidr, the Green One, who like Jhulelal is associated with the fish. The story goes that when Musa (or Moses in the Christian tradition) was travelling with his companion, he saw a dead fish come to life, and jump back into the water. Filled with curiosity, he followed the fish to where the river meets the sea and saw Al-Khidr walking there. Musa travelled with him.

Even Jesus Christ's earlier symbol was that of a fish, not the crucifix that it is today. Why a fish? Because Jesus used to preach on the shores of the Sea of Galilee, and a lot of his followers were fisher people. He used to call them fishers of men. In the Bible, there is another story of Jonah, who doesn't want to follow God's word. One day, he jumps into the sea, and a fish swallows him whole. God tells him that he will continue to live inside the belly of the fish until he decides to listen to his word. The fish, here, becomes a symbol of patience. This idea of a fish swallowing things is quite common even in Hinduism— take, for example, the story of Shakuntala's ring, which gets swallowed and is later found by the cook of the royal kitchen when he cuts open the fish. A similar story is that of Pradyumna, Krishna's son, who is swallowed by a fish and found later in its belly.

Krishna's earrings are fish-shaped because it is a symbol of movement. Krishna is also killed by an arrow with a small metal piece found inside a fish.

Fish are also found in the Mahabharata. In Draupadi's swayamvara, Arjuna pierces the eye of a fish with an arrow to win her. Another story is about Satyavati, the ancestor of the Pandavas and the Kauravas. Fisher people cut open the stomach of a fish to find a girl and boy. They take the two kids to the king who decides to keep the boy, and tells the fisherman to keep the girl. Satyavati is the girl, who ends up marrying Shantanu decreeing that only her children will become kings, to compensate for the cruelty of fate that made her the daughter of a fisherman and her brother the prince. Now, interestingly, when the Pandavas are in exile, they end up taking refuge in Matsya-desha (fish-land), whose king Virata is said to be the descendant of Satyavati's long-lost brother.

The fish is also associated with Shiva. When Shiva and Parvati were conversing about Tantra knowledge, a fish overheard all of this, and consequently was bursting with so much knowledge that he was reborn as a man. There is another story where Parvati yawns while listening to Shiva, and he curses her to be born as a fisherwoman, but soon regrets this curse for now he's lonely on Mount Kailash. Since Parvati can only be married to a fisherman now, Shiva takes the guise of a fisherman to go meet her, woo her, and marry her again.

In a Southeast Asian Ramayana, when the vanar sena fail to get the Ram Setu rocks to float, Hanuman, while attempting to find out what is wrong, meets a mermaid, Swarna Matsya, who commands all the fish to hold the rocks in place.

Varuna, too, over time, becomes associated with the ocean and thus his vahana, his mythic vehicle, comes to be a fish. The fish also has contemporary relevance. For example, in Odia marriages fish are brought to the mandap. The fisher people of Mumbai still cook fish during Gowri Puja, just as Bengalis do during Pujo. Fish mythologies thus are found across history and geography.

Tale 13
....

Cows

When people talk of sustainability, I often think of the Devrahi, a concept in the South, where they keep a grassland empty, where you cannot even allow cows to graze. This was known as Devi's forest, untouched by human activity. When people talk of constructing big bulky temples, I often give them this example. Is a grove more environmentally friendly than a stone structure built to satisfy the ego of man?

There is a story in the Bhagavata Purana that teaches us the importance of sustainable development, a phrase that came about only as recently as 1987, but which has been talked about in the age-old scriptures.

King Vena had plundered the earth, exploiting its resources. The earth, in agony and complaining, goes to Brahma and Vishnu in the form of a cow, asking for help. Vishnu asks the rishis to use the durva grass to fashion a weapon to kill the king.

They then churn the dead body of King Vena in a ritual, and two creatures come out of that churning.

One of the people who rise from the churning is Nishadh, who wants to live in the jungle as per the jungle law. He says, 'I won't farm, I'll hunt and gather to survive.' This word 'Nishadh' would acquire a negative connotation in the nineteenth century and come to mean uncivilized, but its actual meaning has to do with the practice of being one with nature. The other person is Prithu, who says that man should become a householder. He says, 'I will farm and grow, save for my family and myself, and donate to the less-endowed. But I will make sure that need never turns into greed.' Prithu is given a bow, which becomes a symbol of the raja-dharma that balances nature and culture.

The earth, manifested as a cow, becomes anxious about Prithu's desire for development and civilization. This anxiety is seen in the image of Prithu running behind the cow with a bow. They eventually come to an agreement. Prithu says, 'I will not eat you, I will only milk you.' So, he creates an economic enterprise to extract value from the earth, manifested as a cow, without destroying it. Similarly, the cow needs to have enough milk for her calf. The earth was so impressed by Prithu's discretion that she began to call herself Prithvi, daughter of Prithu.

There is another story of King Dileep where this tension between development and exploitation is seen. One day, when King Dileep is protecting the cow, a lion comes to eat the animal. On the one hand you have a starving lion, and on the other you have a cow that needs protection. Within this story, you can see the tension inherent in development.

The lion says, 'As long as I have the forest, with deer, why would I want to eat the cow? But as the pasture land for the cow increases, the forest land for me decreases, and so I am now forced to hunt the cow! When you burn the forest, I have no choice but to eat the cow.'

The king understands that the more cows he owns, the more land he'll need as pasture, and the wildlife will thus spill into his territories endangering their lives and that of the cows. This tension is also seen in the Ramayana when Sita tells Rama not to hunt too many deer.

Of course, the story of King Dileep has a happily-ever-after ending, where the king asks the lion to eat him, and the lion takes the form of Shiva and blesses him. But this ending should not preclude us from discussing the theme—that of need versus greed.

Indian philosophy gives a lot of importance to food and hunger. Feeding has five components: for yourself, for the hungry, for the family, for the ancestors, and for the animal. If you notice the spoon used during yajna, called the uddharani, it is extremely long, so that you cannot use it to feed yourself, only others. But feeding is never at the cost of nature. And most importantly, in these stories, the cow is a metaphor for human livelihood. It is not to be taken literally. But people who do not really care for nature, culture, or religion love to take things literally so that they do not have to really take care of nature or humanity.

Tale 14

....

Shiva

Shiva in Bengal has a big belly, a big beard, and is called Budho Baba. This is so different from the sensuous Shiva of Khajuraho temples or the six-pack hunk of modern art. Shiva has thus undergone a lot of changes over time.

In the Tantric tradition, the body is composed of three parts:

1. Sthula sharira, or the physical body that feels hunger and lust;

2. Sukshma sharira, that thinks, the mental body; and

3. Karana sharira, which includes your property, your title, your reputation. The social body.

Shiva is seen as the destroyer of all three parts.

But the key theme when you want to study Shiva is this: imagine there is a householder who becomes a hermit, like the Buddha or the Jina. Shiva is the opposite of that—a hermit who becomes a householder, the husband of Parvati, and father to Kartikeya and Ganesha. This fierce god, coated in ash, who sits cross-legged on a tiger skin on Mount Kailash, who turned Kama to dust and killed Yama, thus killing both life and death, is now domesticated. He comes down from Kailash to Kashi. Shankara thus becomes the married form of Shiva.

The story of Dakshaprajapati and his daughter, Sati, is perhaps the most well-known story associated with Shiva. When Sati wants to marry Shiva, her father, Dakshaprajapati, rejects this because Shiva is an ascetic figure unfit for civilization. But Sati marries Shiva nonetheless. In a fury, he refuses to invite either Shiva or Sati to the big yajna he is performing. When Sati finds out about the yajna, she is incensed at her father's impropriety, and jumps into the fire. When Shiva finds out about Sati jumping into the fire, he howls in anger, destroys the yajna, and cuts off the head of Dakshaprajapati.

But what is given less attention is the fundamental distinction in the story between tapas and yajna. The purpose of yajna is to provide food, and the purpose of tapas is to destroy hunger. While Shiva inhabits the latter, his father-in-law believes in the former. Only when the two coexist will need never turn into greed.

Tale 15

Apsara

Women are usually associated with marriage in mythology:

1. Women with one husband: Sita, Kannagi.

2. Bhikkhuni or those who do not want to be married: Gargi, Sulabha, Andal.

3. Ganika or those with many husbands—over time, women in this category began to be associated with devadasis: Urvashi, Menaka, Tilottama.

Sunda and Upasunda are asuras, both in love with Tilottama. Tilottama says she will marry the stronger brother, and so the brothers fight, and end up killing each other. Tilottama is thus known to have defeated two asuras without using a single weapon.

While stories of the femme fatale or seductress are more common, we also have stories of the reverse—where a man seduces a woman. When Dirghajeevi rakshasi drinks all of Indra's soma with her long tongue, Indra uses Sumitra, a handsome man, to seduce her, so when she tries to make love to him, Indra can kill her. This story comes from post-Vedic Brahmana literature. It is not known outside academic circles.

There is a story of Agastya, a tapasvi, and Lopamudra,

his wife, who wants him to pleasure her for procreation, insisting that giving her pleasure is his dharma too. This same dialogue takes place in the Puranas between Shiva and Parvati. Here, Agastya muni says he wants to do tapasya and not participate in householder activity.

Urvashi, an apsara, bored with her husband, Pururavas, decides to go back to heaven. Her husband is trying to stop her. It's a very modern story! Pururavas tells her that they have children to take care of, and Urvashi tells him to take care of them himself.

Now, this word apsara is usually translated as courtesan, which has its own colonial connotation. The apsara originates from the Mahabharata, with the churning of the ocean and the creation of amrit. They are independent women, unmarried, adept at the sixty-four arts—conversation, cookery, music, dance, embroidery, architecture, gambling, board games, and so on, and not just sex.

Apsaras are artists in the consummate sense of the word: renaissance women.

Two Epics, One Theme

While the Ramayana and Mahabharata are seen as two separate texts, both of them talk about dharma.

In both there are families—in the Ramayana it is the Suryavansh, in the Mahabharata it is the Chandravansh. The first chapter is about their education and marriage. Then the 'drama' happens leading to exile—thirteen years of exile in the Mahabharata and fourteen years in the Ramayana. Then there is the war, and both end similarly— the Pandavas reaching heaven and Rama reaching Vaikuntha. Structurally, as you can see, they are similar.

Deer appear in both narratives. Rama and Dasharatha chase deer in the Ramayana. Dasharatha is cursed to die while being separated from his son, while Sita is kidnapped when Rama is off to find the deer. In the Mahabharata, both Pandu and the Pandavas hunt deer. Pandu kills Kindama rishi by mistake, aiming for a deer. Whenever a deer is chased, something bad ensues—either Draupadi or Sita is kidnapped, or curses are proffered.

In both there is a period of exile in the forests. When Yudhishthira grumbles about the exile, Markandeya rishi tells him: 'You only got thirteen years of exile. Rama was given a fourteen-year exile! You were exiled because you gambled your wealth away, this is all your fault. Rama was exiled despite not making a mistake, and yet he never grumbled!'

Shiva is also in both epics. Ravana is a devout, if immodest, disciple of Shiva. In the Mahabharata, Shiva appears as a Kirata, a mountain dweller, before Arjuna to give him a shastra, a weapon. In both texts, there is also Shakti puja. Indrajit, Ravana's son, performs Shakti puja, while Rama does so by offering his eyes. In the Mahabharata, before the war, Pandavas pray to the Devi.

Both Sita and Draupadi, the female protagonists of these epics, are ayonija—not born of the womb. Sita is found in a furrow, and Draupadi emerges from the sacrificial fire.

There are stark differences as well. Rama is born to kings, Krishna is born to cowherds. Krishna is the younger child, while Rama is the elder brother.

Tale 17

....

Garuda

Garuda, found in the Vedas, is called Suparna—the one with the golden wings. His job was to carry the pot of nectar from heaven to earth without drinking it. The Vedashala, for the ritual sacrifices, was made in the shape of a bird.

One day when Vishnu asks Garuda out of curiosity, 'Why do you not drink the nectar, or even attempt to taste it?' Garuda replies, 'This is not for me, but for the devas.' Vishnu is very happy with this response and makes him his vahana, his mount. But Garuda, being clever, says in a riddle, 'I will be your vahana, but on one condition: I will only be below you if you keep me above you!'

Vishnu solves this by making a flag with a bird, and so Vishnu is always seen riding the Garuda with a flag of the Garuda above him. Equality is thus established between the god and his vahana.

It is interesting that while in the Vedic period we hear about horses, cows, and snakes, we only start connecting animals with gods—the Garuda vahana, Mooshika vahana, Nandi vahana, Mor vahana—during the Puranic period with the birth of local traditions. These animals also embody strange relationships with each other. Now we can ask why the rat is associated with Ganesha, when there is also a snake across his belly. In the natural world, the snake is supposed to eat the rat, and the rat should eat the modak in Ganesha's hand. But when they are with Ganesha, there is no hunger in them, thus he is able to help the animal conquer hunger. This is shown iconographically, by showing the predator and prey together.

Garuda's mother, Vinata, gave birth to two eggs. But she becomes impatient, and breaks one egg, while letting the other gestate. Aruna is born of the broken egg. Garuda comes from the egg that is left alone. Thus, if Garuda is seen as the sun, Aruna is seen as the shapeless dawn. That is why, in idols, only half of Aruna's body is shown. Since he doesn't have a lower half, he is considered napunsaka—neither male nor female. In some regional versions of the Ramayana, Aruna, in the female form, had sexual relations with both Indra and Surya—Vali is born from Indra, and Sugriva is born from Surya. Garuda, the virile male bird, is treated as a brahmachari, a celibate ascetic serving Vishnu in heaven, as Hanuman serves Rama on earth.

Tale 18

Agni

The Rig Veda, written around 3,500 years ago, has about 1,000 shlokas, out of which 200 are dedicated to Agni, the fire god. In fact, the first verse of the first chapter is dedicated to Agni, since he connects the earth to the sky. The Aryas of the Vedic times did not have temple structures; they would perform the yajna with clay bricks, and once finished, they would burn down the yajnashala, and move on in keeping with their nomadic proclivities. Yajna is thus a portable ritual, unlike the brick-and-mortar temples of today.

The fire is represented by the sun, and sometimes, even the Pole Star, Dhruv Tara. As the ladle-shaped Big Dipper constellation seems to rotate, through the seasons, around a pivot in the sky, it forms the swastika, the pivot being the Pole Star.

One might ask: why is fire so important to the Vedic people?

Humans are the only creatures who can control fire. It is thus a sign of civilization. As long as we are alive, we are warm, and as soon as we die, our body becomes cold, because the fire within us is extinguished. It is, thus, also a sign of the atma. But, more obviously, it represents the household, with a hearth in which cooking takes place. Agni can thus be both wild and domesticated, spiritual and corporeal. This is why in the Vedic period there were three fires—the first for the kitchen, the second for the gods, and the third for the ancestors.

Evidence of using fire to clear land for human habitation is found in the Satapatha Brahmana. (In the Mahabharata, the Pandavas, too, would raze a forest with fire to build their capital city Indraprastha.) Since the fires kept burning as the Aryans moved eastwards, towards Purva, Agni is also called Purohit. So, there is the yajaman—the one performing the fire exchange—the rising sun in the east, and the raging fire between the two. As the Aryans move from the Indus towards Ganga, the Vedas reach their final form.

But the cult of Agni goes even further than the Vedic age. Nala and Neela, the two monkeys responsible for building the Ram Setu, are considered the sons of Agni in the Ramcharitmanas of Tulsidas composed 3,000 years after the Vedas. There is a famous local story where Hanuman is mad at them because he gave them rocks with both hands, but they received it with their left hands, which is considered inauspicious. This is when Jambavan comes and explains to Hanuman that Nala and Neela are labourers, karigars, and that with one hand they receive the rock, and with the other hand they pass it on to the next person, quickening their pace of work.

But while Agni and his progeny are representative of construction and making, they can also be destructive. Dhritarashtra and Gandhari end their life, caught in a forest fire. Gandhari proclaims that they have lived their whole lives, and now they can't escape fire, as they are consumed by its hot flames.

Vedic, Puranic, and Local Stories

There is a Vedic story of three Brahmin brothers, with the youngest being known for his elaborate yajnas. One day, he is returning home with a lot of gifts given by the yajaman, or the patron of the yajna. The two elder brothers get jealous and throw him down a well. The youngest brother prays in the well, and in his imagination sees the leaves as somras and the rocks as gods. The Ashvins come and save him by causing rains to fill up the well so he can swim out. Since he is a rishi, and can't get angry, the gods intercede on his behalf, and turn the two older brothers into a bear and a monkey. These stories were written before the Buddha. There is no Krishna, no Rama, no trace of the Mahabharata or the Ramayana.

One of my favourite Vedic stories is of Rishi Bhrigu's dreams. There are many versions of this. One day, he is dreaming of a human being cutting and eating another human being who is not screaming. But in another dream the man who is being eaten is screaming. He asks his father about his dreams the following day. The father tells him that he has seen the afterlife. In the afterlife, the first vision of the silent scream is a reflection of the trees and plants that you are consuming in this life, consuming you. Because trees cannot scream in this life, you won't be able to scream in the afterlife. Where you have eaten animals, in the afterlife, the animals will eat you. Since animals can scream, in the afterlife you will scream too.

Bhrigu asks, 'How to avoid this?'

His father replies, 'Offer the gods food first, and only what remains after that, must be eaten.' This story is thus used to explain the ritual of feeding the gods, the ancestors, and birds before mealtime in many Hindu households.

As we move forward in time, most of the stories we hear become about Shiva and Vishnu, who are curiously not found in Vedic mythology. These stories come from the Puranic Age that was brewing around 100 CE when the Kushanas ruled from Afghanistan to Mathura. With them came statues—of Durga and the Buddha. The interesting thing is that we find statues of Durga before we find stories of her; the Durga Mahatmya reference comes only around 600 CE, much later!

But even this doesn't give a full picture of the kinds of mythology we are surrounded by, because so much of the stories are local and specific to where we grew up.

I am reminded of my cab driver when I went to Rajasthan. I used the word 'Ramachandra' in the course of our conversation and he asked me why Chandra is associated with Rama when he's a Suryavanshi? I told him the story I had read—of Rama being enamoured by the moon as a child and wanting it in the palace, upon which the queen placed a vat of water in his room so the moon could be reflected in it for Rama. In return, he told me another story that he was told in his village that by banishing Sita from Ayodhya, like the moon eclipses the sun, there was a blot on the Suryavanshis, and this was why Rama was called Ramachandra.

Apart from local variations of popular stories, there are also local stories that you don't find anywhere else. Pabuji's tale comes to us from Rajasthan. It is said that Lakshmana was reborn as Pabuji. Surpanakha too was reborn as a woman to whom Pabuji is about to get married, but the marriage never takes place.

From Madhya Pradesh comes the story of Prithviraj Chauhan and his daughter, Bela, who is married to Brahma, the son of Jaychand. But in this story, Prithviraj is not a hero because he doesn't accept his son-in-law because of complications based on caste and tributes.

In Maharashtra, there is Khandoba who kills the demons Malla and Mani. If you go to a Khandoba temple, you can see the god's association with Shiva. In Pandharpur, Maharashtra, Vishnu is worshipped as Vitthala, a local form. As per local temple lore, Krishna goes to a devotee's house to meet him. The devotee says he will first serve his parents before coming to him. He takes a piece of wood and throws it towards Krishna telling him to stand there and wait till his parents have finished eating. This is why Vitthala of Pandharpur is always standing like he's waiting. Thus local stories are different from Puranic stories, which in turn are different from Vedic stories.

Tale 20

·····································

Karma

You have probably heard the phrase 'Karma is a bitch'. What is implied here is that karma is a form of justice. This is not true. Justice is a European concept based on a human living one life between birth and death, during which he receives justice, whether temporal or spiritual. In Abrahamic religions, God is the judge.

'As you sow, so shall you reap' is not karma. That's a line from the Bible. Krishna always maintained in the Bhagavad Gita that one must perform actions without worrying about the consequences, 'Phal ki chinta mat karo.' You may sow something, but you may get something else altogether, or nothing at all, and that's okay.

People often think of the Bhagavad Gita as a motivational talk that led to the Pandavas winning the war. Yes, the Pandavas won the war, but look at what happened in the war. All their kids were killed—Bhima's son Ghatotkacha, Arjuna's son Abhimanyu, Draupadi's son Upaveda are all killed. So, what kind of victory is this where all your progeny are murdered?

If you have read the Gita, Krishna never gives a guarantee, though that is what we, as humans, crave—which is why we buy into the cults of occult godmen who assure us that we will surely get money, meaning, and power. The Bhagavad Gita only helps us cope with uncertainty.

As the idea of rebirth becomes important during the Upanishads, the meaning of karma changes from the purely yajna-based ritualistic duties to something metaphysical. The idea of burial versus cremation becomes important here—those who will be born again are burned, and those who won't, like the enlightened matha gurus, will be buried. Cremation and the pouring of ashes into the river are related to the concept of rebirth.

In the Mahabharata there is the story of Shantanu and Ganga. When they were getting married, Shantanu vowed that he would not ask her any questions at any point, promising unfettered freedom. But slowly, over the course of the marriage, Ganga kills each of the seven children she begets from Shantanu; he is forced to remain silent due to the vow he gave her. But when it comes to the eighth child, pushed to breaking point, Shantanu stops her as she is about to drown the child.

From one perspective, you can say Shantanu is the good person here, saving the child, and Ganga is the bad one. But because Shantanu is a mere human, his knowledge is limited, while Ganga, a goddess, knows her children were Vasus in their previous birth, and were cursed to be born on earth; the only way in which they could regain their immortal status was through a very short life. She was thus only attempting to liberate them. So, there is a bigger story involved. In saving the eighth child Ganga tells Shantanu, 'You haven't saved your son. He will not marry, and will raise someone else's child. He won't become a king, but will take care of someone else's kingdom. And in the end, he won't even die the death of a noble warrior at war. He will be killed by a napunsaka.' So, who was right in this story? The idea of rebirth makes things complicated. Karma makes it difficult to judge the right from the wrong, the good from the bad, as we have to factor in actions from previous lives.

Similarly, most people would find the story of Ajamala in the Bhagavata Purana unfair. Here is an awful human, who on his deathbed calls out to his son 'Narayana'. But only because that is also the god's name, and this was his last word, he gets to live in Vaikuntha in the afterlife. Is this fair?

Fair or not, it is karma.

Tale 21
....

Justice

In the jungle, there were two plants growing close to one another—a banana tree with smooth leaves, and a berry shrub which had a lot of thorns. One day, when there was a brisk breeze, the berry shrub's thorny branches rubbed against the smooth leaves of the banana tree tearing them. If I ask you whose fault this was, what would you say?

The banana tree for standing next to the thorny shrub? The berry shrub for having thorns? Or the wind for swaying the branches of the shrub so they rubbed against the banana tree?

The truth is the wind will blow as that is its nature, and the banana tree and berry shrub grew where they were entirely by chance. They had no choice in the matter. But human observers are obsessed with holding someone responsible—we need a hero, a villain, a victim. We need victims so we can be saviours. But in nature, no such impulse exists. This gets even more muddled with our modern conception of justice, which replaces the tradition of karma.

Most of us are aware of the very famous story of Gandhi being kicked out of the first-class compartment of a train in South Africa because he wasn't white. A similar story exists elsewhere, with Chanakya, when he goes to Pataliputra to meet the Nanda king. The king gets upset because he finds Chanakya ugly and egoistic (different stories give different reasons for the king being upset), and he's kicked out of the palace. Chanakya vows revenge. Both of them, Chanakya and Gandhi, are thrown out and decide to take revenge for the injustice shown towards them. There is a similar story in the Mahabharata where Dhrupad thinks Dronacharya is inferior to him, and sends him packing; so Dronacharya decides to seek revenge on him.

In all these stories, the idea of justice has been spun into stories of revenge for the sake of dramatic quality. An eye for an eye, a tooth for a tooth, like the Bible says.

The image of justice as weighing scales, both sides being equal, comes from Egypt. In India, there is the story of Sibiraj found in Hinduism, Buddhism, and Jainism. Once, when he sees a hawk about to catch and devour a dove, he decides to save the dove. When the hawk asks him what he will eat if the dove is saved, Sibiraj offers him his own flesh. He cuts off flesh from his body and puts it on one pan of the scales, with the dove sitting on the other pan. This is called Tulabharam. But the dove is so heavy that Sibaraj has to keep cutting off his flesh till his body disappears. Did Sibiraj do the right thing by interfering in nature's pattern with his idea of justice?

There is another Tulabharam story of Narada asking Krishna's queens to give him Krishna himself as a gift. The women refuse but agree to giving Narada something equal to Krishna's weight. Satyabhama takes this literally and puts all her jewels on one side of the balance, with Krishna on the other side. But Krishna turns out to be heavier! Rukmini takes one leaf of the tulsi plant symbolizing all her love for Krishna, places it the empty pan, and it becomes heavier than Krishna. The idea of love turns out to be heavier than the reality of wealth. How does one factor in ideas of love and forgiveness in the world of justice that seeks evidence. Can love be proven using material evidence? Can forgiveness be confirmed using measuring tools? Can a good actor not fool us by pretending to repent?

This story tells us the importance of measuring being inherent in justice. Justice is about what we can measure and not what we cannot. This makes sense because what kind of a court gives judgement without evidence? But then we must also ask, what about justice for things that can't cough up evidence? Rukmini's love cannot be measured, yet it weighs more than all of Satyabhama's jewellery. Indian mythology values that which cannot be measured as much as that which can be measured. Life is not just about measurable things. The idea of rebirth draws attention to the non-measurable that will always confound the idea of justice so critical to modern myths.

Tale 22

North–South–East–West

We are able to identify the north through the help of the Pole Star or Dhruv Tara. The Pole Star can be found by using the Great Bear or the Big Dipper constellation that rotates around the Pole Star.

A famous story associated with the north is of the genesis of Ganesha's elephant head. In a rage, Shiva cuts off the head of a boy who blocks his passage into Parvati's cave. Parvati, now angry with Shiva, asks him to bring the boy back to life, announcing that the boy is her son that she created on her own to give her company while Shiva was away meditating. Shiva asks his ganas to go northwards and bring him the head of the first animal they find. It happened to be an elephant, and, thus, Ganesha, the elephant-headed god is born.

If the north is associated with stability then the south is associated with movement and flux. Dakshina Kali, a form of Parvati, makes the journey to Shiva from south to north. Dakshina Murthy, a form of Shiva, sits in the north, looking down south at Kali, who comes from south (Dakshin) and is also called Dakshinayani, daughter of Daksha. It can be said that in the case of Ganesha's body, the lower or southern part, is created by Devi with clay, and the upper or northern part, the elephant head, is fixed by Shiva. Ganesha, thus, is seen as a composite of the two directions and two ideas, Shiva and Shakti.

Movement between these directions becomes significant in Indian mythology. The north to south trajectory is seen in the story of Agastya who travels south, taking with him the mountains and rivers. Therefore, southern rivers are called Dakshina Ganga and southern mountains are called Dakshina Kailash. Buddhism and Jainism also travel from north to south. Kartikeya, mad at his father, Shiva, is said to have moved southwards, which is why, even today, he is popularly revered in South India as Murugan.

But there are also inverse stories, with a south to north trajectory, like the story of Madurai Meenakshi. A queen in search of a husband, she goes north to find Shiva, and bring him back with her, to the south. Another such story is associated with Kanyakumari (which literally means 'unmarried woman'), the southern tip of India. In olden times, unmarried women were known to be powerful. For this reason, the gods wanted Kanyakumari to remain unmarried, but she had her heart set on marrying Shiva and so they set a date for the marriage, and Shiva was told to get there before sunrise.

But on his way south, in the middle of the night, the gods made the sound of a cockerel that signals sunrise. Shiva thought this meant that the sun had already risen, and that he was late. Dejected, he cut short his journey and returned to where he had set out from. This angered Kanyakumari who emptied all the food prepared for the wedding into the ocean. This is why, people say, the colour of the ocean in Kanyakumari, where the Bay of Bengal meets the Arabian Sea, is unique. The colourful sand there is also created from wasted wedding food.

There are also other stories of people moving from south to north like Shankaracharya, who coined the term 'Dravida'; Vallabhacharya; and Ramananda.

Moving west to east, like the Aryans moving from Indus to Ganga, becomes an important signifier of civilization. When you face the east, you face the rising sun, and so the east represents growth. Does one want growth or permanence in life? The north-east corner of the household, between the Pole Star and the rising sun, is thus associated with continuous, sustained growth.

In the Satapatha Brahmana there is the story of King Videha Madhava who charges east with fire, which basically means he burns the forests on his way. This was written around the time the Aryans were moving from the Indus in India's north-west towards the Ganga, burning forests to make way for human settlements and farming.

Another story is of Dirghatama rishi, born blind. His wife, frustrated with him, tells their children to throw him into the Ganga which flows eastwards. Floating, not drowning, he reaches King Bali who, unable to procreate, asks if Dirghatama rishi will produce an heir with his wife, Sudeshna. She gives birth to three children, who established three kingdoms—Anga, Vanga, Kalinga, or Bihar, Bengal, Odisha respectively.

In the Bhagavata Purana, when Jarasandha burns down

Krishna's house in Mathura, Krishna becomes a refugee and travels west to Dwarka. The west is associated with rishis like Bhrigu, Jamadagni, Parashurama. It is here, on the west coast, that Parashurama's axe stained with the blood of greedy kings caused the oceans to retreat and reveal the Western coast.

But these notions of north–south–east–west are not just mythological or symbolic. Pre-Vedic Harappan cities have followed this north–south–east–west grid pattern perfectly in the construction of all their cities, as a sign of city planning, and, thus, civilization.

Tale 23

....

Christianity

How many non-Christian readers of this book have made the mistake of wishing their Christian friends 'Happy Good Friday'?

Good Friday was when Jesus Christ was crucified; three days later, on Sunday, he was resurrected—the festival of Easter celebrates this. Thus, Good Friday is not a day of celebration.

The Bible itself is in two parts—the Old Testament with Jewish stories and the New Testament with Christian stories. The Gospels contain the story of Jesus Christ, written years after his crucifixion, by Matthew, Mark, Luke, and John, each presenting Jesus in a different light.

This idea of resurrection and sacrifice is very common in Abrahamic religions (Judaism, Christianity, Islam). One of the most famous stories in the Old Testament is of Abraham (Ibrahim in the Quran). God asks him if he truly believes in him, and when Abraham replies 'Yes!', God asks him to sacrifice his own child for him. Abraham takes his son to the top of a hill to sacrifice him; just before he is about to kill him, God intervenes, happy that Abraham trusts him entirely. He gives him a goat instead, to sacrifice. This is how Bakra-Id, celebrated by Muslims, originated. But while God saves Abraham's son, in the Old Testament, in the New Testament, we are told God sacrifices his own son to pay for the sins of humanity.

But Christianity, like any religion, isn't a monolith. It has its own divisions. Under the Roman empire there was a Church in the East, in Byzantium, and one in the West, in Rome. Then, the Church underwent a Protestant Reformation in the sixteenth century, as a movement against the Catholic Church. In America, there is another group called the Mormons. Much like this, Islam, too, has fragmented into multiple Shia and Sunni factions, some bitterly persecuted by fellow Muslims.

Just like there are divisions, there are also commonalities. Take, for example, the Biblical story of Mary that is also found in Islamic lore where she is called Mariam. When she is pregnant with Jesus, she feels thirsty and hungry in the desert. In response, the dates from the date palm bend towards her, for her to pick and eat them, and the water from the oasis rises up for her to drink. Jesus, in her womb, assuages her discomfort by saying he will be out soon. In Buddhism there is a similar story with Mayadevi giving birth to Siddhartha Gautama, who will become the Buddha. She reaches out to the branch of a tree that bends down for her to hold. This image of a woman holding on to a tree and giving birth is very common.

If you look at the prophets in Islam, their names are similar to that of their Christian counterparts: David becomes Dawood, Solomon becomes Sulaiman, and Noah becomes Nooh, a prophet who built the ark to survive the Great Flood. This story, of the Great Flood, is similar to the story of Manu, but in Manu's story there is no reason given for the pralaya. It is seen merely as a part of the cycle of life. In the Bible and Quran, the flood is about God's wrath.

Tale 24

....

Easter and Holi

Easter is about regeneration, celebrated in the spring that has emerged from winter, and giving way to summer. It is associated with the vernal equinox (in the northern hemisphere the vernal equinox falls on 20 or 21 March), the midpoint between the two solstices, when the length of the day and the night are the same.

During the vernal equinox, a zodiac is seen just before the sun rises. This zodiac shifts every 2,000 years. From 2000 CE, it is the Age of Aquarius. From CE 1 to 2000 CE, it was the Age of Pisces. From 2000 BCE to CE 1, it was the Age of Aries. And before that it was the Age of Taurus. In the zodiac, Taurus is the constellation known as Pleiades, or Krittikas in Sanskrit literature.

In the Satapatha Brahmana, the Krittikas constellation is associated with the vernal equinox, suggesting this Vedic scripture was written before 2000 BCE, during the Harappan Civilization! People pounce on this and say that this is because the Satapatha Brahmana, and thus the Vedas, were composed during the Harappan Civilization. But that does not fit in with other information in the Vedas (the absence of cities, presence of horses) and DNA evidence. This could only mean that an observation from Harappan times kept getting transmitted through vestigial memories till it was finally written down around

800 BCE. It implies a continuity between the Harappan and Vedic age—in that the words came much after the experience.

Easter is celebrated on the Sunday following the full moon after the spring equinox. This is very interesting because while the solstice and full moon are natural phenomena, Sunday is a man-made, constructed idea, created in Babylon. Easter is celebrated around the time of Shivratri and Holi, and it's no surprise that all these festivals are about rebirth and regeneration. Holi celebrates the rebirth of Kama Deva, who was killed by Shiva. Jesus Christ is crucified on Good Friday, and on Sunday he is resurrected as the Son of God. It was in Germany that Easter's goodness was associated with rabbits and eggs. Some connect Easter with Ishtar, the Babylonian goddess, whose beloved Dumuzi rises from the land of the dead in springtime.

....

The Celebration of Spring

Everyone has their own gods, their own religions, their own subsects, but the birth of spring is celebrated throughout India. Easter and Holi are also, in a sense, spring celebrations.

The coming of spring is celebrated under different names across India: Poila Baisakh in Bengal; Panna Sankranti in Odisha, where they make a juice out of mango spiced with pepper. There is Bihu in Assam, which is also celebrated in Cambodia, Bali, Thailand, and Vietnam. This means this celebration might have something to do with Buddhism, which spread between the third and thirteenth centuries CE from India to Southeast Asian countries.

In the South, Vishu is celebrated in Kerala, where the first thing one must see in the morning is one's reflection in the mirror surrounded by gold, rice stalks, and the amaltas flower, which looks like a shower of gold. Gold, as you can see, becomes a symbol of abundance. In Punjab, too, you have Vaisakhi. So, from Punjab to Kerala, Thailand to Tamil Nadu, what is this cultural unity we possess celebrating the same idea under different names and traditions? Shall we call it religion, or culture? Maybe Hinduism, or simply Indianness? Some people will be astute enough to notice that the

Mesha Sankranti is on 15 April while Spring Equinox is three weeks earlier around 21 March. This difference is because when the Indian calendar was created 1,500 years ago, the Mesha Sankranti (entry of the sun in the zodiac of Aries) happened during Spring Equinox. But the sky has changed in the centuries since then. The movement of the zodiac along the horizon known as 'Precession of Equinoxes' was not known to ancient Indian astronomers. This is also the reason why we celebrate Uttarayana on Makara Sankranti (15 January) instead of 21 December, the winter solstice, which is three weeks earlier.

....

Tirth, the Ford

With the arrival of the Industrial Revolution the handicrafts industry was destroyed, instead becoming part of a high-end, elite category of art. This was one of the inevitable trade-offs of development. Similarly, Indra's thunderbolt, his vajra, comes from the bones of Dadichi rishi; someone had to give up their body for this powerful thunderbolt to exist. In order to build Indraprastha, the Pandavas had to destroy the Khandava forest. There is a constant tension between life and death, development and extinction.

One needs to acknowledge the nature of this world where one is both the eater and the eaten. It is the fundamental human condition. Buddhism calls it dukkha.

Understanding that gives perspective to a world that is as random in its violence as it is in its kindness. Jainism created a concept for this—kaivalya or omniscience. When artists were asked to make a representation of this concept, they decided to put the image of a Jain tirthankara on a mountain with four heads, Chaumukh, to see everyone and everything—their insecurities, their fears, their hopes.

Have you noticed how, in Jain temples, the twenty-four tirthankaras all look the same? This is because they have all risen beyond their personal differences and desires—

for development, for exploitation, for betterment—that mark them as individual beings. It is only from unique symbols like the tree or the yaksha that we are able to identify them.

The word tirthankar comes from 'tirth', which means the ford—the shallow part of the river where one can cross it. It is not a bridge; it is not man-made. It is the natural connection between two shores that must be discovered. This is also the genesis of the wheel symbol, where the eye of the wheel is you, and the periphery of the circle is everyone you want to connect with, and the spokes are the connection. Another word for this connection is yog. The disconnection is called vi-yog.

Self-help, Indian Style

Generally, we associate the word 'success' with having achieved something. The word success doesn't translate well in Hindu texts. Instead, what we find is the idea of purushartha, which means having led a meaningful life. Success comes from Maslow's theory of needs—from survival to physiological needs to self-actualization. I have always had an issue with this.

The concept of Ikigai, too, I find perplexing—to find the intersection between what you're good at, what you can monetize, what makes you happy, and what people need. But like one of the comments on the Teatime Tales webcast pointed out, where do personal relationships figure in this framework?

Rama is not achieving anything, he is going from one place to another, flowing with the chain of circumstances. He reacts to circumstances. Similarly, the Buddha didn't 'achieve' nirvana, he was just looking for a way out of discontentment. It seems from the texts that it is often the villains, Duryodhana, for example, who are obsessed with this idea of planning and plotting.

The idea of success comes from the strong influence of Greek individualism—for a person to become something in the course of their life. This is reflected in today's thought processes, too; to become rich, famous, victorious, powerful—this is considered success. I have met these rich and powerful people, and they are just as insecure and pained as everyone else. People often don't want money but what money brings—freedom, or respect, or comfort. Money is the means, not the end.

Remember, what is unique among all these self-help books that are being churned out a dime a dozen is a focus on the 'self'. Confucianism emphasizes culture over nature, on becoming a refined human being through the conduct of ceremonies. Daoism is about being one with nature, privileging that over culture. In Western philosophy, we see the tension is between the individual and the collective. South Asian ideology, with a strong focus on rebirth, has the tension between nature, and culture, and the self.

In Hindu mythology, there is ahankara and atma. Ahankara is Me! Me! Me! Atma is recognizing that you exist in an ecosystem of people, and understanding how to see others and how others see you. Here, individualism is not isolated in a vacuum. It is embedded in the larger fabric of society. More than getting the self somewhere, it is more about letting go of the self so that the self can recognize it is nothing without others and others are nothing without the self.

Time and Place Change Stories

The Hindustani word 'naukar' comes from the Mongols, 800 years ago. They used the word to describe a paid soldier, not a servant, its current meaning. Similarly, 'chakar' meant a clerk, a person who works for money. These words meant professional salaried people. Before these Persianate and Central Asian ideas came, Indians didn't work for salaries, but according to their jati or family vocation.

Just as the meaning of words changes over place and time, there are often geographic variations of the same story.

When Tulsidas retold the Ramayana in Awadhi, the local language, he faced a lot of opposition. But look at the text today, and see how it is Tulsidas's and not Valmiki's Ramayana that is performed in the Ramlila. It's not a translation but a reimagination where Rama is god-on-earth and not just the venerable hero that he is in Valmiki's telling.

If you look at the Buddhist Ramayana you will quickly realize it's not the one Hindus are familiar with. For one, there is no Ravana here. Here, the prince is told by his father, the king, that his stepmother is planning to kill him, so he is sent to the forest for fourteen years, because, according to astrological predictions, the king will die in fourteen years; the prince needs to come back to reclaim the throne. But fate is unpredictable, the king dies after only nine years. Bharata, Rama's brother, then goes to the forest to bring him back. Rama refuses since he had given his word to his father that he would stay away for fourteen years. Bharata requests his paduka, his footwear, so they could be kept on the throne in his stead until his return. And that is it! The Ramayana here is a story of the integrity of a man who keeps his word even if it means spending more time in the forest rather than claim his throne. He trusts his brother to have integrity too.

In Jain Ramayanas, Rama is non-violent—it is Lakshmana who kills Ravana.

Similarly, there is a very unique addition in the Odia Ramayana, Baidehi Bilasa, that is not seen anywhere else. When Rama goes to the jungle in search of Sita, the rishis, who want to comfort him, come to hug him. But Rama refuses saying only Sita can touch his body. All the rishis feel bad about this. So, Rama tells them, 'In this birth only Sita can touch me. But I will reincarnate as Krishna in the next birth, and all the rishis can reincarnate as gopis, and we will dance together.'

Krishna

In the Vedas there is mention of a cowherd. But we do not know if this is Krishna or not. It is only in the Mahabharata that we first see him, not as a cowherd, but a statesman. There is no Radha or Yashoda here. He directly enters the story during Draupadi's swayamvara. So, the Mahabharata only contains stories from the second half of Krishna's life till his death because of Gandhari's curse.

It is only in the appendix to the Mahabharata, the Harivamsa Purana, that we first get the story of Krishna's birth and childhood. This genre grows and becomes the Bhagavata Purana. The second part of Krishna's life comes first in classical Indian literature. Isn't that interesting?

In South India we also get a lot of stories of Krishna's marriage—stories of Satyabhama and Rukmini, especially in Telugu literature. The story of Satyabhama killing Narakasura in anger comes from Andhra Pradesh. In Sangam poetry, Mal and Pinnai might be referring to Krishna and Radha respectively. There's a greater focus on his adulthood in the South, whereas in North India, the stories focus more on his birth and youth.

Krishna is given supernatural powers in the later lore. For example, when his guru, Sandipani, asks Krishna to rescue his dead son as guru dakshina, Krishna goes to Yamlok to get him back. Rama of Ramayana on the other hand, does not have such supernatural abilities, to bring back people to life. Similarly, we don't see shringar bhava, or madhurya bhava with Rama. Rama, therefore, does not get called purna-avatara, or the complete manifestation of God on earth.

Another interesting distinction between Rama and Krishna is that Krishna is *not* a king, he's a service provider, a sarathi. This is because the Yadu clan to which Krishna belongs, was cursed by Yayati that they would never become or beget kings. It is believed that the Yadus formed the first democracy—they used to have sudharma, a council of local leaders, since they didn't have kings. As per one theory, Krishna was a lover of democracy and, he rejected Kansa, Duryodhana, Jarasandha, and other monarchs or dictators. He even defeats Indra, who represents the monarchy. For him, the ideal was governance through consensus. So, while Krishna comes across as the ideal democrat, Rama is the ideal monarch. Colonial writers insisted that democracy comes from Greece but there is evidence that some form of democracy existed in ancient India too, as indicated by the story of Krishna.

Krishna goes by Rannchor in Dwarka. This is because when Jarasandha attacks, burns, and destroys the city of Mathura, Krishna escapes the battlefield and flees to Dwarka as a refugee, leaving the battlefield, determined to live and fight another day. This counters the hyper-masculine Rajput narrative of great warriors dying valiantly on the battlefield, choosing death over dishonour.

But the way we see Krishna depicted today is almost at odds with how he is supposed to be seen. Krishna is supposed to be dark-skinned. Another name for him is Ghana Shyam, as dark as rain clouds. But nowadays Krishna is made from white marble as opposed to black stone. In television series, too, the actors playing Krishna are often fair as milk. Not all changes are based on wisdom.

Rangoli as Metaphor of the Mind

In the Upanishads there is a famous word, Brahman. This is different from BrAhman, which refers to the priest community, which is different from BrahmA, who is the creator of living beings, a member of the Hindu trinity, as per the Puranas. You can divide the word Brahman into two parts: Brah means expanding, and Mann means mind. It is about the expansion of the mind. Now the question here is: how does one expand the mind?

Indian philosophy is often divided between purusha and prakriti, humanity and nature. What distinguishes prakriti from purusha is manas—the human imagination.

Let's look at the rangoli or the kolam, a common sight in India, to understand this. In Punjab and Uttar Pradesh rangoli is called chowk purna, in Madhya Pradesh and Rajasthan it is called mandana, in Odisha, West Bengal, and Assam it is called aripana. In a rangoli there are dots, and then lines to connect the dots. This can be understood as a metaphor—given a page full of dots, everyone will join the dots differently. This means that the information received (the dots) is the same, but how you process this information into patterns (the lines) is unique to you. We see the same world, but we react differently to it. The more information, the more dots, the more complex the processing, or the patterns; infinite dots, infinite patterns.

Our mind is, thus, much like the rangoli in the aangan (courtyard) of our household.

Similarly, remember stars are natural, constellations are not; we have connected the stars to make the patterns, dividing the skies into parts we can understand. We are humans because we can find these infinite patterns, but we can also appreciate other people's patterns, absorbing aspects of theirs into ours. This is Brahman. The infinitely expanded mind. Fear, desire, and ignorance crumple the mind and create the ego—Aham.

Tale 31

The Different Buddhisms

Buddhism, like any religion, isn't a monolith. The old school of Buddhism, Theravada, is found in Thailand, Sri Lanka, and Myanmar. In Theravada Buddhism nothing is permanent—where there is desire, there is sadness. Meditation and silence thus become important. Here, you will find big sculptures of the Buddha, in various mudras, either standing, sitting, or sleeping. Though historically we know that the Buddha had pulled out all his hair, in these sculptures we always see a mound of hair on his head. Sometimes, in Southeast Asia instead of hair, we see fire.

For over 500 years after the Buddha's death, he was only represented as a tree, a handprint, his crown, or parasol. It is only when the Greeks introduced Buddhist sculptures, that his face started being made, and people added hair, because the Greeks considered it inauspicious to be bald.

In China, Korea, Japan, Taiwan, Singapore, and Hong Kong, we see another variant of Buddhism, Mahayana Buddhism, which is very different from Theravada Buddhism. Here, Bodhisattvas are often seen with the Buddha. And there are multiple Buddhas living in infinite Buddhist realms, not just the one Buddha. Here, it is about praying *to* the Buddha, unlike Theravada where they meditate *as* the Buddha. In Mahayana Buddhism, there are chants, for many Buddhas, and Bodhisattvas, including Amitabha Buddha and Avalokiteshvara Bodhisattva. In China, there is even a female Buddha, Guanyin. Bodhisattva statues have many hands and many heads. Avalokiteshvara always has his head lowered so he can hear the pleas of the earth's people. Wisdom is personified as a goddess called Tara. Tara's image becomes very important as it integrates the female energy into Buddhist thought, which was otherwise rather masculine.

In Tibet, Bhutan, and Sikkim, another form of Buddhism, Vajrayana Buddhism or Tantric Buddhism, is practised. It came about in the eighth century CE. Here there are sexual and violent forms and sculptures, too, like the Yab-yum sculptures of male and female figures engaging in sexual acts, and the fierce Heruka sculptures.

There are 550 stories of the previous lives of the Buddha in the Jataka tales, where he is seen as a flower, a monkey, a soldier, a merchant, etc. But, interestingly, in not a single tale does the Buddha take the form of a woman. In Theravada Buddhism, women were always considered inferior. The Buddhist female nun, a bhikkhuni, is a reluctant addition. In Vinaya Pitaka, the rules for monks, there are more rules for female monks than male monks. The oldest statue of Tara, who comes around 800 CE, can be found in the Ellora Caves, holding a lotus in her hand.

There is also Padmapani, a form of Avalokiteshvara,

holding a lotus, that can be found in Ajanta. If you notice, Padmapani is striking a feminine pose, the tribhanga, where the body, instead of standing straight, is S shaped—bent at the neck, waist, and hips. The story here goes that the Buddha was giving people knowledge, and one bhikku stands up and pleads, 'You have explained so much but I have understood nothing.' The Buddha picks up a lotus, and looks at him. When the bhikku just looked in the direction of the Buddha, that was enough. He achieved nirvana. What cannot be achieved by words, can be achieved by sight. All communication is not verbal.

Buddhist and Hindu tales and traditions can have their similarities because of the cultural interchange that took place. The Shyama Jataka, for example, has a story of a king hunting a deer, and hurting a human child instead, by mistake. This child was taking his parents on a pilgrimage when he was wounded. Where else have you heard this story?

This is very similar to Shravan Kumar's story where the blind parents curse King Dasharatha after he kills Shravan Kumar by mistake—that he too will die separated from his child. But in the Shyama Jataka, the parents showed compassion, and when their compassionate tears fell on the child, the child was brought back to life, and their eyesight was also brought back.

But the link between Hinduism and Buddhism is not just relegated to myths. Buddhist and Hindi iconography, too, have similarities. The oldest Indra and Brahma images and sculptures are always found with the Buddha. The concept of Indra sitting on a white elephant, Airavata, comes from Buddhism. In the Vedas, Indra is sitting not on Airavata, but on a chariot steered by two brown horses. The idea of Indra being associated with rain comes much later. Vedic Indra is thus a warrior god, not the rain god that we consider him to be today. In the Vedas, Paranjaya is the rain god.

A statue in the Bhaja Buddhist caves, on the Mumbai–Pune highway, showing a man sitting on an elephant, is the first time we see an idol depiction of Indra, with women playing the tabla around him. The oldest image of Lakshmi is found in Sanchi's Buddhist stupa. The oldest image of Brahma is found in Deogarh in UP, in a Hindu temple, seated on top of a lotus flower, not attached to Vishnu's navel, as shown in contemporary iconography.

Tale 32

Surpanakha

This story of Surpanakha comes to us from the coastal regions of Tamil Nadu through shadow puppetry. The shadow puppetry travels from here, through sea-merchants, between 300–1300 CE, to Southeast Asia where it is still very popular. We are told that Surpanakha's husband's name is Vidyut Jihva. We know from some other versions of the Ramayana, that Ravana, Surpanakha's brother, had accidentally killed his brother-in-law, Vidyut Jihva. In repentance Ravana tells Surpanakha that she can live in Dandakaranya and any man she wants is hers, which is where she meets Rama and Lakshmana.

There is another story about a quarrel between Mandodari, Ravana's wife, and Surpanakha. Their husbands get involved, and at one point, Vidyut Jihva eats Ravana who is now inside his stomach. Ravana uses his charm to tell his sister to take him out, but she says that if she has to take him out, she will have to cut open her husband which would kill him. Ravana tells her that if she takes him out, her son, and not his son, will rule Lanka. This excites her, and so she cuts open her husband and pulls her brother out of his stomach. Of course, Ravana being Ravana reneges on the promise saying that only his son, Indrajit, will be heir to the throne.

So, Surpanakha swears vengeance and grooms her son, Jivaka, to kill Ravana. There is a fascinating story of Jivaka meditating in the forest, when a cosmic sword appears before him. It just so happens that Lakshmana who is passing that way sees the sword floating in the air and grabs hold of it. While attempting to swing it back and forth to test it out, he cuts off the head of Jivaka by mistake. The news reaches Surpanaka, who is initially angered. But then she later rethinks her strategic revenge on Ravana when she realizes that Rama and Lakshmana are two beautiful kshatriyas with a sword that can kill Ravana and thus avenge the death of her husband. So, there is a very complex moment here, where on the one hand she wants to avenge the death of her son, but also wants to use the murderers of her son to avenge the murder of her husband. This story comes from the coastal South, and it might have something to do with the matrilineal tradition here. It is often said that it was Rama who brought patriarchy to the South. This is again just a theory.

....

Marriage

Indian mythology is filled with stories of women as property. That is why a woman is supposed to live with her father before marriage and her husband after marriage. But in many tribes, as also in the story of Arjuna going to Chitrangada's and Ulupi's house, the man lives with the woman's family. Their child is called Chitrangada's child or Ulupi's child, not Arjuna's child. There were thus different conceptions of marriage that were based on caste and power.

In the Vedic Age, there were eight kinds of marriages:

1. **Prajapati Vivah:** When a man asks, and the father gives his daughter's hand in marriage. The father here is doing a favour to the son-in-law.

2. **Brahma Vivah:** When the man doesn't ask, but is still given the daughter. The groom here is doing a favour to the father, which is why dowry is expected. Draupadi's marriage is considered a Brahma Vivah, though some also consider it a Prajapati Vivah.

3. **Rishi Vivah:** A hermit is given a woman to marry, along with a cow and a bull, so that they can give up ascetic practices and set up a household. Some

people say dowry comes from here and not Brahma Vivah. The marriage of Renuka and Jamadagni is a Rishi Vivah.

4. **Deva Vivah:** When a girl is given as dakshina, a fee, and for service provided by the groom.

5. **Gandharva Vivah:** A love marriage, like that of Shakuntala and Nala–Damayanti.

6. **Asura Vivah:** Where a girl is bought, like Madri, Gandhari, and Kaikeyi.

7. **Rakshasa Vivah:** When the girl elopes or is abducted. Like the story of Rukmini and Krishna, or the story of Bhishma carrying away the Kashi princesses Amba, Ambika, and Ambalika.

8. **Paishacha Vivah:** When a girl is forcibly made a wife, by making her pregnant.

There are also stories of queer love and marriage. In the Padma Purana, there is a story of two men who were very poor, Sumedha and Somavat, and were also desperate to get married, but no family was willing to give their daughters to them in marriage. They would tell the two men, 'If you had a cow in your house, we would get our daughter married to you.' It just so happens that there is a queen Somantini, who, every Monday, would give cows to newly married couples. So, the two men decide to go to her, as a couple, with one of them dressed as a woman, to get the cow. They decide that the next day, the other man would dress as a woman, and this way they would have two cows, and get married. The queen doesn't realize this, but the gods, angered by this, decide to turn the man acting as a woman, into a woman, and thus Somavat becomes Somavati. But what happens next is interesting. The people in the story are resigned to this new development. Friends become a married couple with two cows. This story, for me, is about same-sex love, or at least signals a clear comfort with that idea. A similar story like this is also found in Tamil traditions.

There is also the story from the many tales of pilgrim sites in the Puranas of princess Brahmani and her friend Shudri. Both their marriages are fixed. But it so happens that there is a man who is cursed, and in order to get over the curse, he must touch the breast of a woman. If he is truly repentant, she will lactate. He places his hand on the princess's breast and she lactates, but this news spreads, and her engagement breaks off. Her friend, comforting her, says, 'If your engagement is broken, then so will mine!' The story ends with the two women living together in the forest, forever. What do you make of such a story?

....

Writing

Two thousand eight hundred years ago in Mesopotamia, modern day Iraq, there was an Assyrian king, Ashurbanipal, who had a huge library of 30,000 clay tablets. Text in the cuneiform script would be imprinted on clay and then dried in the furnace. Initially, these clay tablets were used for accounting, but later they were also used for recording stories. This library contained some of the world's oldest stories.

In China, around the same time, there were bones, on which the Chinese pictographic script was carved, similar to the hieroglyphics on Egyptian walls. These were used by oracles to communicate with gods and spirits. The Indus Valley Civilization script is, however, shrouded in doubt and controversy, and we are not sure whether the inscriptions found there even constituted a script or were merely symbols. As of now, there is no evidence of the fact that writing was happening in India around this time. Ours was not a civilization that wrote. We listened and memorized.

Books came very late to India. For millennia we were an oral culture. The first part of Hindu scriptures is called shruti, to be heard. The latter part of the scriptures is rooted in darshan, to see. It is, thus, not about reading, it is about being immersed in a world of sound and sight without worrying about transcribing it.

Even the story of how the Vedas come to be reflects this. When the Saraswati River dried up, there was severe drought. The Brahmins were dying, and, thus, the Vedas which they had memorized were facing an existential moment. Needing someone to remember the Vedas (as opposed to writing them down), Ved Vyasa manifested himself. He listened to and organized the Vedas into four texts—Rig Veda, Sama Veda, Yajur Veda, and Atharva Veda.

The stories of Ganesha writing down the Mahabharata that Vyasa was dictating come much later. Similarly, the stories of the vanar sena writing Rama's name on rocks must also, by this logic, belong to a later period. But even in this later period, the texts were written to aid easy memorization—in rhymes and couplets, with meters and rhythm. The sutras, or the poems, thus, come before the shastras, or the prose. The Dharmasutra, for example, comes much before the Dharmashastra.

The oldest script that has been deciphered in India is the Brahmi script. We see the Brahmi script for the first time in Ashoka's edicts. In South India, there was South Indian Brahmi which people believe predates Ashoka's Brahmi.

Writing was first adopted by Buddhists and later Hindus, and it became widespread during the Gupta period. They would write on palm leaves, which couldn't withstand the ravages of time and so we can't read them today. Copper and stone plates were also used, usually for property and land deeds. The script was adapted according to the material on which it was being written. In the South, where palm leaves were being used, the script became more circular, without sharp corners, so the leaf would not tear. In the North, when they were writing on bricks and metal, the edges of the alphabets were sharper. As the written word grew in importance, so did scribes and poets.

Then, with the Turkic incursions into India in the twelfth century CE, paper and pen, kaagaz and kalam, are introduced. Thus, the book becomes important, replacing the oral traditions that existed before. So, you have a massive regional literature emerging now because these stories were finally being written down, and then travelling the world, through Arabia to Europe.

Islam rose in Arabia and was clearly influenced by ancient Mesopotamian ideas where writing was key for priests and accountants and traders. So, holy books had to be written.

Muslims believe that during Ramzan, the ninth month of the Islamic calendar, all holy books of the world are written: the book of Abraham that has been lost, the book of Moses (Torah), the book of David (Psalms), the book of Jesus (the Gospels), and the Quran.

Tale 35
....

Varnas and Jatis

When you meet people in rural India mostly they often ask about your caste and village of origin.

The Vedas speak about four varnas—those involved with the knowledge economy (Brahmins), the land economy (Kshatriyas), the market economy (Vaishyas), and the service economy (Shudras). Now, if you take the Kayasthas or the scribes found in North and East India, they were Brahmins who were not involved in temple activities, they were associated with the accounts of kings, collecting taxes, and other financial matters. The temple priests thus began to see them as not-Brahmin enough, and slowly these categories became less sharply defined and often contentious.

The Vedic word varna is very different from the common word jati. Varna is a collection of jatis. But the varna categories are not watertight as there are four varnas but thousands of jatis. Jatis were initially constituted as occupational groups who practised endogamy (marrying within the group), and thus wouldn't break bread, or share their daughters in marriage with those from outside the group—the roti–beti system. Then came hierarchy, when one kind of labour was seen as better, and more valuable. To this was added another layer of purity, which conveniently did away with the dignity of labour, so people doing 'impure' jobs were seen as having 'impure' bodies, to be shunned. Concepts of untouchability became mainstream.

Indian villages came to be designed in circles, with the 'impure' jatis populating the fringe. (The concept of purity is also associated with women, with menstruation, and giving birth.) This idea of endogamy comes *not* from the Vedic period, but only 2,000 years ago, and this has been corroborated with genetic data showing signs of endogamy coming only in the post-Vedic period. What exactly happened earlier than 2,000 years ago is disputed. We know that Chinese pilgrims who came to India 1,500 years ago refer to communities who were considered impure. Even some Vedic verses refer to impure Chandalas. So the idea of untouchability is far older than endogamy, giving caste a very complex origin.

This mapping of jatis to varnas also becomes messy. Only with Brahmins is it more or less clear. With Kshatriyas, the land-owning class, it gets confusing, for in South India it was the Brahmins who owned land. Krishna, for example, was a cowherd; which varna would you place him in? Musician and weaver communities in the South, who served in temples, were called Brahmins as they became prosperous. But while class is related to money and power, caste has the additional connotation of purity.

The nudge away from generational professions towards merit comes 200 years ago with the introduction of the civil service examinations—the Chinese invented it over 1,500 years ago and the British brought it to India less than 200 years ago. The idea of merit is now taken seriously, something that would come to the fore only after the Industrial Revolution. But of course, this doesn't mean we can forget caste-based prejudices, which have leaked into the new millennium, because violence and discrimination linger. At the same time, we must not let Hinduism be equated with caste because then saying anything good about Hinduism makes you casteist. Basically, avoid extremes. Extremes are toxic.

Tale 36

Hara–Hari

When you close your eyes and think of the image of Shiva, what are the first few things that come to mind?

When I asked the people who tuned in during the webcast of Teatime Tales, here were some of the answers:

- Crescent moon
- Matted hair
- Trident with damru
- Third eye
- Tiger, deer, or elephant skin
- Ganga
- Cobra
- Ash

Now do the same about Vishnu.

- Crown with a peacock feather
- Curly hair
- Weapons
- Dark skin
- Garland
- Sandalwood paste
- Yellow silk cloth (Fun fact: the yellow dye would come from feeding cows mango leaves, and filtering the yellow urine for the pigment.)

What is the fundamental difference between these two images?

Shiva's images are related to that of the tapasvi, living with nature, keeping animals away with his ash and trident, tying his matted hair with the jute of a banyan tree, scaring away animals with the damru.

Vishnu's images are that of an inhabitant of a village, living among people—a goldsmith for the crown, a weaver for the silk cloth, associated with farming and industry. Using the flute and conch-shell requires training. Not so for the rattle drum.

With Shiva you will see the rudraksha, or a seed, but with Vishnu you see garlands of flowers, and the tulsi all in bloom. One represents potential (Hara), and one represents realization of the potential (Hari). Even their choice of consort is representative of them—Kali associated with wilderness, is with Shiva, while Lakshmi, representing family and civilization, is seen with Vishnu.

But, interestingly, we only see photos of Shiva with his family—his wife and two children. Are there photos of Vishnu with Lakshmi and their children? The popular avataras, Rama and Krishna, are not portrayed with their children.

Creation Myths Across Cultures

This is an Inuit story, part of the mythology of the Arctic region. It is said that a man gives his only daughter, Sedna, in marriage to a seagull. Married and off, she misses her father very much, and so the father arrives in a boat to take her back. On their way back, all the seagulls attack them. The father, scared, begs them to allow him to take his daughter back for a few days, but the seagulls refuse his pleas. The father, frustrated, pushes his daughter off the boat, but she hangs onto it, hoping not to drown and die in the frigid waters. The father cuts the fingers of his daughter, and she drowns and transforms into a goddess. From her cut fingers in the ocean, all kinds of creatures emerge under the water—seals and walruses, fish and sharks, all considered the daughters and sons of Sedna.

The important part of Sedna's creation myth is that she is not seen as the creator of the sea world, but just the animals who populate it. Similarly, Brahma did not create our world, but only the people who populate it, as opposed to the Abrahamic religions where God created the earth, the heavens, and beyond. In Hinduism, the Purusha creates time. Prajapati makes 720 elements—360 days and 360 nights, to give form to time. The yajnashala, the sacrificial fireplace, too, has 720 bricks to indicate creation of time.

In the Brihadaranyaka Upanishad, there is a conversation about what humans can live without. We can live without eyes, for there are blind people, without hearing, for there are deaf people, without speech, for there are dumb people, without genitals, for there are eunuchs. What we cannot live without is food and air.

Among the Santal tribe of East India, the origin myth involves an earthworm digging earth from the seabed and putting it on top of a tortoise shell. It sounds similar to stories in the Brahmana literature where the earth is placed on top of the tortoise Akupara. Which story came first? There is no way to really know this because so many of these stories travelled orally first before finally being written down.

Temples

When people ask me why Hinduism thrived in India, as opposed to Buddhism and Jainism which slowly waned, the biggest reason I can think of is that Hinduism celebrated life with its rich tradition of devadasis or temple dancers, prasad, song, and theatre in service of the deity in shringar, who gets boat rides on moonlit nights, and is made to see the town during the Rath Yatra.

Think of Jagannath in Puri, Odisha, where the sweets are made on one side of the temple, and then distributed on the other side, in Anand Bazaar, the bazaar of happiness. Jagannath is a very worldly deity, who takes naps, wears different clothes, and eats different food for different seasons. He falls ill for fifteen days a year, during which he is allowed to rest; his painting is prayed to during that period. He is reborn with a new statue replacing the old one every twelve years, wearing different layers of cloth representing different human attributes, veins, muscles, etc., reconstructed with cloth and herbs and wood. Rebirth and joy are thus demonstrated through ritual. There is even the element of performance, where Lakshmi gets angry for not being taken along with Jagannath on the Rath Yatra and closes her doors on him.

Temples are where people come together. It is a

composite space meant for celebration. Of course, today people speak about temples as spaces for meditation, and this is a Buddhist influence, since it is darshan that was seen as the primary reason for temples.

Temple building in India happens in full flow between 800–1200 CE. To understand how temples came about, we need to understand their former incarnation—the Buddhist stupas. After the Buddha's death, his relics, his bones, teeth, etc., were distributed, and each relic was placed in the earth under a mound of mud, with an umbrella and a flag. This became the stupa. This is, of course, deeply ironic because the Buddha lectured on the impermanence of the body, but his followers were fighting over his remains, much like what would happen later with Kabir.

But, slowly, a hall was built around the stupa, the chaitya, and the act of walking around the stupa became commonplace. Later, viharas were made for the monks to live in. This influenced the Indian ideal of a temple. In the centre is the garbha griha, which unlike the Buddhist ideal of death, references the womb. Here it is life that is important. A kalash and a flag were placed on top of this. A parikrama mandal was built around this, and the mandapa was created for people to sit and do darshan. Around the temple, there were the agraharams or places for Brahmins to stay, much like Buddhist viharas.

Oldest original temples were actually in open air: rocks, rivers, caves, mountains. Many such rocks were enclosed in temples, under Brahmin influence. Even today, much of Indian worship takes place without any temples. Sacred spaces are created before the ritual and wiped out after ritual. No trace is left as in the ancient yagna-shala.

Tale 39
....

Devas and Asuras

In the Vedic period, the world was divided into swarglok, bhulok, and the space in between the two, antariksh. The concept of subterranean pataal didn't exist. This comes much later, in the Puranic period, along with the concept of asuras living under the earth.

Today, we talk of devas as good and asuras as bad, but this wasn't always the case. In Iran, in fact, it is flipped— Ahura (~asura) Mazda is their god and Div (~deva) is the demon. The Iranian Avesta and the Vedas studied side by side show the linguistic similarity; we don't know when or why this flip of meaning occurred.

The devas who live in swarga have Brihaspati (Jupiter) as their guru, while the asuras in pataal have Shukracharya (Venus). Jupiter is associated with rational thought, while Venus is associated with intuitive thought. The day, the waxing moon, the lengthening days of summer are linked to devas while the night, the waning moon, and the shortening days of winter are linked to asuras. They are two powerful forces working together. It is *not* a good versus bad binary, but a force and a counter-force.

It is the Puranic stories that come later that solidify the notion of good versus bad, with the Puranic gods slaying the asuras—Shiva kills Annakasur, Kartikeya kills Taraka, Durga kills Mahisa, and Vishnu kills Hiranyakashipu.

These stories, thus, become an archetype that goes something like this: the asuras perform enough penance to become powerful, praying to Brahma for immortality. Brahma rejects this, and the asuras and Brahma reach a compromise, where they are given some other power, and are thereupon suffused with megalomania. Eventually, all the asuras are brought down by the gods after finding a loophole in the boon of Brahma.

Asuras come to be associated with mortality, placed next to devas who are associated with amrit, the elixir of immortality. Asuras also possess Sanjivani-vidya, the ability to resurrect the dead. Both devas and asuras have a common father, Kashyapa. But Aditi is the mother of devas and Diti is the mother of asuras.

What happens in this muddle is rakshasas often get confused with asuras. Rakshasas live in forests while asuras live under the earth in pataal. Rakshasas do not value yagna while asuras value yagna which is why Shukra is their guru. The enemy of rakshasas is the yagna-performing rishi. The enemy of asuras is the amrit-stealing deva. So, beware while telling stories, asuras and rakshasas are not the same.

....

The Ka'bah as Metaphor

Shiva is called Thakurdev by many tribes in India. He is seen as the god who taught them to cultivate and eat rice, from the times they were hunting and gathering. Friction emerges here, too, between the wandering tribals and those who settled down, because the latter, like us, believed in private property and boundaries, while the wanderers believed in no such thing.

This dichotomy is seen even in the 4,000-year-old images of the pharaohs of Egypt, with criss-crossed hands. In one hand there is a farmer's flail, and in another a shepherd's crook. The latter is used to domesticate animals, and the former is used to dehusk grains. Harivamsa, the appendix of the Mahabharata, gives us stories of Krishna's childhood for the first time. Associated with the cow, he always has a crook on him (this image is mostly found in South Indian temples), and Balarama, his brother, associated with farming, always has a plough.

In the Bible, there is a story of Cain and Abel, sons of Adam and Eve. Cain, a farmer, kills Abel, an animal herder. Here, too, you see the rivalry between the farmer who has settled and the herder who has animals that eat whatever fodder is available. A similar story can be found in the Quran, where Cain is Kabil, and Abel is Habil.

Cain lives in a house of stone, and Abel lives in a house of cloth, a tent, and thus his life is nomadic. The Ka'bah, the stone room or original house of prayer in Mecca, is covered with a black cloth. This is the union of the fighting brothers—the nomadic (the cloth) and the farming communities (the stone).

In Hindu mythology, this tension is shown in the story of a snake and an eagle, the former representing settlements and the latter, nomadism. This is why when Vishnu is resting, he is on the snake, Ananta, and when he is travelling, he is on the eagle, Garuda. Vishnu makes opposing forces work with each other. He is therefore called the preserver.

....

From the Vedas to the Puranas

In Vedic mythology, Shiva and Vishnu are absent. While the word Shiva is found in the Rig Veda, it is used as an adjective. The word Rudra found in the Rig Veda is associated with howling winds; this is not Shiva as we know him today. We even find the name Vishnu but he is merely Indra's brother, who takes three steps across the sky to mark time and thus becomes Trivikrama, the conqueror of three worlds.

One of the few connections then between Vedic and Puranic mythology that continues till this day is rebirth. Though it is only mentioned sparingly in the Rig Veda, it becomes a fuller concept by the time of the Upanishads. Even the avataras, previously associated with Prajapati, become crystallized with Vishnu. It's almost as if a radical reconstruction is taking place.

Vedic stories, which we rarely talk about today, have a different flavour altogether. These stories are not popular perhaps because they are vague; you really don't know what they are trying to communicate.

Take, for example, the story of Aditi found in the Brahmanas where she feeds the Purvadevas, and eats the leftover food from which she begets children—the Adityas. The second time she is hungry, and so eats before serving the Purvadevas, and this time she begets three children—one child is aborted, one becomes the king of all living creatures, and one child is the king of the dead—Marthand, Manu, and Yama respectively (the unborn, the living, and the dead). What could this story possibly be about?

In the Puranas, Indra is the god of rain and thus freshwater, and Varuna is the god of the sea and thus saltwater. Indra is associated with war and movement while Varuna is associated with peace and stability. Indra drinks Soma, an ephedra. Varuna is associated with Sura, alcohol.

Now, why did the stories change?

To answer this, we have to look at history, specifically between 3,000 and 2,000 years ago. In the Vedas, there is no reference to South India. The older Dharmashastras always portray India as being between the Indus and the Himalayas, and the Vindhyas. The idea of Aryavarta being from the mountains to the sea comes in the newer Dharmashastras. It is only with Ashoka's edicts that the first mention of the Cheras, Cholas, and Pandyas are seen. Vedic stories were written in the northern regions. Puranic stories were more diffuse. This journey from North to South is exemplified in the Ramayana.

So, the first change we see is the Brahmins moving from North to South—rishis like Agastya, Gulatsya, move South. Dirghatama is talking about Anga, Vanga, Kalinga. Gautama rishi is associated with the Godavari. Indeed, it is in the South that we first get the description of Vishnu as Perumal. References to Radha as Pinnai, Mathura as Madurai, and Durga as Kottravai exist in ancient Sangam literature composed in old Tamil. Ramanuja, Sankaracharya, Madhavacharya, Ramananda, Vallabhacharya all come from the South. As the religion was becoming more diffuse, it also had to adapt to its local stories, including them within its fold.

Then, there is the rise of Buddhism and Jainism, and with that the concepts of rebirth and renunciation get popular sanction. This also forces Vedic stories to change and focus less on the ritual of yagna and more on ideas such as maya, moha, and moksha, i.e., delusion, attachment, and liberation.

It is in the Upanishads, between the Vedic and the Puranic period, that we get the first clear story relating to rebirth when Nachiketa asks Yama, 'Is there life after death, or is death the end?'

The Stories We Tell

Tale 42
....

Don't Turn Around

The story of Sakshi Gopal in Odisha is very interesting. Once, when a Brahmin was travelling like a pilgrim, hapless, tired, and worn out, with nobody willing to help him, a young man showed up and offered assistance.

In return, the Brahmin told the man to come to his village, and he would give his daughter's hand in marriage to him for his kind deed. Days later, when the man actually showed up at the village to seek the Brahmin's daughter's hand, the Brahmin refused saying he had promised no such thing. The Brahmin insisted that the man bring a witness. The man, realizing that there was a Krishna temple near where the Brahmin had promised him his daughter, goes to the temple and innocently asks Krishna to come and be his witness. Krishna agrees on one condition, 'Don't ever turn around to confirm if I am following you or not. Just believe that I am behind you!' Then, exactly as one would expect, while they are walking, Krishna behind the man, the anklets of Krishna stop making a noise because they are travelling through soft mud. The man, in fear, turns around, and it is at that moment that Krishna turns to stone.

This 'piche mud kar mat dekho' or 'don't turn around' is a very common trope. The Ambaji temple in Gujarat has a similar story. During the Teatime Tales webcast, when I told this story, there was a flood of responses from the audience of local gods and goddesses with similar stories, like Danteshwari Mata in Chhattisgarh.

But this isn't limited to India. The story of Orpheus and Eurydice in Greek mythology comes to mind. Orpheus was a great musician whose music would make the world simper. One day, his wife Eurydice dies, and in grief he goes to the land beyond, the land of the dead, to get her back, and while getting her back he is told not to turn around, believing that she is following him. But alas, he does, and she returns to the land of the dead.

Even in the Bible there is the story of God telling Lot that when he is escaping the doomed cities of Sodom and Gomorrah he must not look back. But Lot's wife turns around and becomes a pillar of salt.

There is even a Japanese story of the First Man and the First Woman. When the First Woman dies, the First Man tries to bring her back to life, and he is told not to look back but he does and his wife turns into a monster and becomes a ghost. This is called an archetype. This same archetype of not looking back is also found in a Zen story, but here there is a nice moral twist to it.

A monk is travelling with his disciples. As they are walking along, they come to a river. The water is shallow so the monk says they can wade across, and their wet clothes will dry as they continue their journey. But, suddenly, a courtesan beckons to the monk, asking him to take her to the other side, for she has a patron waiting for her there. She can't get her clothes wet, and so she asks if the monk could carry her. The disciples object, saying they cannot touch such a woman, but the monk agrees to carry her, much to the shock of the disciples. When they reach the other side the courtesan says the boys lost an opportunity to carry a beautiful woman and leaves. The disciples keep mulling over the encounter, wondering why and how the monk, who told them to maintain celibacy and stay away from women, could carry the courtesan on his shoulder. After a while, they are unable to keep their thoughts to themselves any longer and confront the monk. For a second, the monk doesn't know what they are so worked up about. The disciples get agitated and remind him of the courtesan. The monk replies, 'That woman? I left the woman on the banks of that river. Are you still carrying her with you in your head?' This adds a layer of metaphor to the act of looking back—the students now realize they were burdened by memories of the past.

Tale 43

The Earth and the Sky

Across cultures there is a story of the earth and the sky being one, but slowly, when a child is born, that child separates the two. This is found in the Rig Veda where Prithvi and Dyaus are separated by their son Indra. It is also found in Greek myth, where Uranus and Gaia are separated by Cronus. In Polynesian mythology, too, Maui separates Rangi and Papa, the earth and the sky. There is a nice touch of beauty here, where to clothe the earth you have plants, and to clothe the sky you have stars. In Egypt it is the opposite—where the earth is a man and the sky is a woman. Isn't this similar to Kali being found on top of Shiva in iconography?

But while the three worlds exist, there is also movement between these worlds. There are so many stories of people going up and coming down. For example, in the Ramayana, there is a story of Trishanku who wants to go to heaven but Indra stops him, and he is stuck between the earth and the sky. Yayati, too, goes to heaven and is thrown out from there.

This movement between heaven and earth is connected to the yajna, where descendants perform a yajna in the name of the deceased. This use of yajna as a vehicle between these worlds is seen in the story of King Indradyumna. After dying and spending time in swarglok, he is suddenly asked to return to bhulok, because no one in bhulok now remembers his deeds. He is told that if he wants to come back to swarglok, he must ensure that he is remembered i.e., people perform a yajna in his name.

When he reaches the earth he is shocked to see that everything has changed. The buildings he built have vanished, the temples he built are no longer to be seen, and those who benefited from his largesse as a king have died. No one remembers his name.

He tries to find the oldest living being and is routed to an old man, who then points him towards an owl, who directs him to a stork, who then sends him off to a tortoise. When he asks the tortoise if he remembers anyone by the name of Indradyumna, the tortoise replies, 'Yes. He built this lake!'

This perplexes Indradyumna because he did not build this lake. The tortoise explains, 'My grandfather never lied! He told me that this king spent his entire life giving away cows in charity, hundreds of thousands of cows. As these cows left Indradyumna's city, they kicked up so much dust, it created a depression in the ground. So, when the rains came the water collected in this depression and turned it into a lake. Now this lake provides sustenance to innumerable plants and animals and worms and weeds and fishes and turtles and birds. So, we remember the great King Indradyumna, whose act of charity resulted in a lake which for generations has been our home.'

Indradyumna was pleased, and so were the gods

who welcomed him back to swarglok. As Indradyumna rose to heaven, the irony did not escape him—he was remembered on earth for a lake that was unconsciously created, and not for the cows that were consciously given. He benefited not from things he did, but from the impact of things he did.

Tale 44

....

Jungle Law

The Matsya avatara comes in the Vishnu Purana, where a small fish comes to Manu, pleading with him to save him from the big fish. The Vishnu Purana was written 1,500 years ago. A thousand years before the Vishnu Purana, the Satapatha Brahmana has a similar story of Manu and a fish, but this story has no mention of Vishnu. It is just a story of matsya–nyaya, where the big eat the small—the jungle law.

Slowly, as local traditions enmeshed with Vedic stories, Vishnu as a god emerged, but the idea of saving the fish from jungle law remained in various iterations of the story.

Just as jungle law is found in Hindu mythology, the reversal of this jungle law is also found. For example, it is said that the Vijayanagara empire was founded in a place where the rabbit finally confronted his predator, the fox. Similarly, the Sringeri Math was made when the frog, usually a victim of the snake, was found sitting under the hood of a snake. Another manifestation of this is the Pandavas, who, with only seven armies, defeated the Kauravas, who had eleven armies. Despite being weaker, they won the war!

This idea of predator and prey, winner and loser, keeps showing up. Chinnamastika is a Hindu goddess of the

Tantric tradition who embodies both these concepts. She cut her own head off and with her severed head drinks the fountain of blood pouring from her neck. This is representative of nature where you are both prey and predator.

But there is also a philosophy that undergirds jungle law that is outlined in the story of King Dileep. Once, when a tiger was chasing a cow, King Dileep tells the tiger that he will protect the cow, and if the tiger wants, he can eat him instead. But the cow asks the king, 'What happens after you die? Ask, instead, why the tigers of the jungle are coming into your kingdom to eat the cows. It is because you have burned the jungle to make your kingdom—you have taken land away from them. So, where do they go to hunt for food? What is more important: the wild or the domestic animal?'

A sense of co-dependence, of ecological destruction, and food pyramids is implicit in this story. There is a story associated with the Yellowstone National Park, where the authorities decide to kill all the wolves. But suddenly they notice that all the grass is disappearing. With no wolves to control the population of the deer, the deer were grazing extensively, causing the loss of grassland. Nature has its own way to create balance. Humans may call it cruelty.

The Stories We Tell

....

Star Wars and the Ramayana

Have you watched *Star Wars*? The film franchise follows the paradigm of the monomyth, where the main protagonist, the hero, the nayak, triumphs over odds and transforms into an extraordinary being. In *Star Wars*, Luke Skywalker makes a long journey in the course of which he meets a damsel in distress and magicians, fights off monsters, and so on. Finally, when he comes back home, his journey has transformed him into a hero and he is unable to relate to any of the people he left behind. This story is anchored in Greek mythology, specifically the *Odyssey*.

Now, in a few ways there is some connection between *Star Wars* and the Ramayana. There it is Darth Vader, here it is Ravana. Princess Leia is like Sita. Hans Solo is like Hanuman. The guru, Obi-Wan Kenobi, here is Vishvamitra and Agastya muni.

When Rama comes back from his exile, he is a different person having experienced both life in the forest, and the war with Ravana, but the people in Ayodhya are the same. The transformation angle isn't very potent or obvious in Hindu mythology, where scenes swirl, and do not necessarily build. Character transformation is mostly found in Greek mythology.

But I must also introduce a cautionary note here.

While it is fun, and indeed illuminating, to look at the similarities between Hindu and Greek stories, one must also see where they diverge. Take the *Iliad* and its comparison with the Ramayana. While it is true that both the *Iliad* and Ramayana end on tragic notes, where the victors are not happy despite having won, they also radically differ. In the *Iliad*, Helen isn't kidnapped, she goes on her own to be with Paris. In the Ramayana, Sita is abducted. In the *Iliad* they travelled by boat, while the Ramayana had to build a bridge over the sea. In the *Iliad* all the neighbouring kings helped, while in the Ramayana, Rama only had the vanar sena to support him.

Old stories often inspire new stories. For example, *Kalevala*, an epic poem in Finnish folklore, is about a great hero and musician who could make one swoon and sleep to his music. This influenced J. R. R. Tolkien while he was creating the world of *The Lord of the Rings*. Myth inspired literature, one ancient, one contemporary.

This is another reason we must learn our mythology as we travel forth to foreign lands. Because when we are there, and we hear their folklore, sometimes, their stories will feel familiar, and the cultural threads connecting the two distant cultures will be established, separated by oceans and, often, time.

For example, look at this story, and think if it rings a bell.

Once, on an island there was a fisherman. One full moon night, he saw beautiful women dancing by the shore of the sea. He quickly realized that these are special creatures that emerge from the seals in the sea on full moon nights, play on the beach, and then become seals again and go back into the water. He falls in love with one of the women, and so steals her seal-skin so she cannot turn back into a seal again, and is trapped in the land of humans. She eventually gets married to him, and follows all her marital duties, including birthing children. One day, when her children are playing in the sand, they come across a seal-skin and bring it to their mother who, looking at it, begins to weep in remembrance of her life as a seal. She puts on the seal-skin and runs back into the sea, never to see her husband or children again.

Isn't this story similar to Ganga running away from Shantanu? In Japan, too, I heard a similar story but instead of a seal, the Japanese speak of foxes. In Germany, the wife is a swan. Of course the moral of this story, at least in India, gets warped over time. It becomes a warning to not fall in love with women from a higher caste or class. They will break your heart.

....

Vaad–Vivaad

In China, culture takes the form of chopsticks that have been used for almost 2,500 years ago. In Europe, culture takes the form of forks and knives, which came into use only 500 years ago through the Byzantine empire. And, in India culture is about eating with the right hand, because we use the left hand for ablutions. Each of these are historically determined cultural practices that have then been fortified by myth.

For example, a unique thing about Indian food habits is that we mix food—dal with rice, for example. The thali or sadhya is how it is eaten here. Europeans have different meal courses. The Chinese have the bowl concept where food is made bite-sized. The bowl in India is a sign of bhikshu or sanyas, even begging, and not nourishment as it is in China.

But even within India, the differences are vast. For example, the Panch Pir concept is found in Rajasthan, central India, Bengal, and the South, and each part of India has a different interpretation of it. Towards Uttar Pradesh, these are known as the five people who protected the cow. In Bengal, the Panch Pir will help your boat stay afloat. In Shia Islam, it refers to five important members of the founding family of the faith: Ali, Fatima, Hussain, Hasan, and Prophet Muhammad.

But as we note these differences, we should also note the possibilities of intersection, and where they begin differing from one another. For example, sagotra weddings between cousins is seen as a distinctive South Indian tradition, anathema in the North. But in the Mahabharata, considered a quintessential Gangetic plain saga, there are so many sagotra weddings—of Pradyumna, Krishna's son, to Rukmini's niece of Krishna's sister to his paternal aunt's son, Arjuna, and of Arjuna's son to Balarama's daughter. How does one explain this?

The reason for this difference is that we find different ways of living around this world. But the moment we believe that one culture, one way of living, is better than the other, ahankar or pride sets in. When people speak about vegetarian food being better, it comes from pride, and a false notion of purity. We have always been a society of both vegetarians and non-vegetarians, including during the Vedic and Harappan period. No culture is better or worse, each one has its inherent strengths and weaknesses.

We must thus remember that we are a nation of discourse, vaad–vivaad. Look at Shankaracharya who propounds Advaita Vedanta, then Ramanujacharya who disagrees, propounding Vishisht–Advaita Vedanta. Then Madhvacharya comes along and theorizes Dvaita Vedanta. Chaitanya Mahaprabhu popularized Bheda–Abheda Vedanta. These four are not in agreement, but they are four gurus with four valid points. And that's okay because our nation is a venn diagram, and it is

in this maddening riotous flux of diversity—vibhinn–
vaad—that we exist. Let us focus on conversation or
sam-vaad not debate or vi-vaad.

Is the Ramayana a Romantic Story?

I have a theory that when one comes across a new person, four things come to mind, either consciously or subconsciously:

1. Can the person in front of me devour me—are they a predator?

2. Can I eat this person—are they prey?

3. Will they steal my food—are they a rival?

4. Can they collaborate with me—are they an ally or a mate?

Let me tell you a story that moves between these questions.

The *Epic of Gilgamesh*, one of the first poetic texts in the world, was written around 4,000 years ago in Mesopotamia, present-day Iraq. Gilgamesh was a strong and powerful king, half-god, half-human, but he also caused a lot of trouble in the lives of his people who begged the gods to intervene, and send someone to deal with him.

For the first time, he is confronted with his equal, Enkidu, a man from the jungles, and when they meet, they fight as rivals to establish domination. But at the end, realizing that he has finally found his equal, Gilgamesh becomes friends with Enkidu. It is when Enkidu dies that Gilgamesh realizes that he too, like Enkidu, will die one day.

But he wants to be immortal, and so sets off on an odyssey. During this journey, he meets an immortal man who tells him, 'You want to conquer death! First see if you can conquer sleep. Don't sleep for seven days and I will show you the secret to immortality.' Gilgamesh accepts this and begins praying but at the end of the first day itself he falls asleep, waking up only after the seventh day. The basic story here is that one is destined to be mortal. But to allay Gilgamesh's worries, the man gives him an herb to become young again. But it so happens that a snake steals this herb from him, which is why it is said that snakes can shed their skin. So, even as the gods are immortal, the science of rejuvenation lies only with the snakes.

Now, while we look at most of mythology as asking the first three questions about predator, prey, or rival, I want to try and look at those same stories through the fourth question, through love.

The Ramayana, for example, is primarily seen as a story of valour and not love. But its beginning betrays this logic. The text begins with Valmiki hearing the lament of a female bird whose lover has been killed by a hunter. In shoka, or sadness (from where the word shloka comes), Valmiki composed this poem about separation. So, doesn't this make the Ramayana the quintessential story of virah, or separation from the lover?

Similarly, the story of Adam and Eve, at least in Islamic mythology, doesn't end with them being expelled. Adam was cast out to Serendib, which is perhaps Sri Lanka, or perhaps India, and Eve was exiled to Jeddah. They were separated and began longing for one another, filled with virah ras, till they finally met in Mecca. There, the angel Jibreel teaches them to how to build a house, how to farm, and teaches them how a man should love a woman, how to be beautiful for and with each other. The story of the first sin is actually a story of love and togetherness.

My favourite folk love story however is that of Sohni–Mahiwal, where in order to meet her lover, Mahiwal, Sohni floats across a river by holding onto a pot. But a jealous person replaces the baked pot she is using with an unbaked one, so the next time she tries to cross the river, the pot turns to mud and she drowns.

Tale 48

....

Unconditional Love

In James Bond you find a character who is willing to die for queen and country—the idea of a young, sexy man, who, in his heart of hearts, loves nothing more than his country. But the country doesn't belong to him; there's no personal relationship, and yet he is willing to give up his life for her.

Let's look at another story from medieval England, that of King Arthur who is about to get married to Guinevere. The king asks his biggest landowner to bring her from her house to the palace, but her escort, Lancelot, ends up falling in love with her. The to-be queen isn't aware of the landowner's love for her. Like Bond's love for his country, the landowner's love feels like the purest form of unconditional love, like the story of Tristan and Isolde; love that doesn't demand to be loved back. In some versions, Lancelot and Guinevere do become lovers behind King Arthur's back, and the tragedy is that they have to hide their feelings for the sake of social propriety and respect for the king.

But what is implicit in this unconditional love is equality. It is somewhat similar to the concept of courtly love (or raag darbari in Indian mythology), which started around the tenth to eleventh century in Europe with stories of King Arthur and the Knights of the Round

Table. The concept here is fidelity to the court and radical equality because there can be no head of the table if the table is circular.

The opposite of this would be possession, the belief that you are entitled to someone's love. The Bible chastises such thoughts, as can be seen in the story of Prophet Nathan chastising Jerusalem's King David because he murdered the husband of Bathsheba, whom he wanted to marry.

Indian mythology stories abound with themes of union and separation—how the parijat flower will bloom only in the night because of its being jilted and thus separated from the sun-god, or how the sunflower will always face the sun, and bloom in its light, in union with it.

Buddhism eschews stories that talk of romance. For example, there is no love story between Yashodhara and Siddhartha. When he comes back as the Buddha he only sees her as a woman, not his wife. Although, even much later, in Mahayana Buddhism we begin to see Tara's statue, here, too, there is no love or shringar bhava, something that will populate Hindu thought later, especially during the Bhakti movement.

Tale 49

Culture and Civilization

I find the question 'are you cultured?' a very silly one because everyone comes from a culture, and is, thus, so to speak, cultured. When we start domesticating and controlling nature, culture begins. The first sign of society is, thus, the hearth, the fire. The ability to control fire exists only with humans. Then, we began to shape rocks into weapons—shastra, the weapons to hold, and astra, the weapons to throw. Combining stones and sticks to form bows, hammers, and maces was a huge invention.

Then came the cave paintings. Why were these marks made in the Bhimbetka caves in Madhya Pradesh, dating all the way back to 8500 BCE? We don't know what these scratch-mark symbols mean, or if they are even meant to mean something. But there is a clear desire in these humans to express thoughts. Not meaning necessarily, but like the scribbles of a child—just to express themselves. This desire isn't seen in animals. With the ability to create art, we begin to connect it to meaning.

In the Rig Veda there is a prayer, Asatoma Sat Gayama, 'When I express my imagination, it becomes sat from asat.' This is the birth of knowledge and the arts. The arrival of Saraswati is the beginning of humanity. Civilizations form when humanity and culture advance over time, when society becomes layered, standardized, and holds sway over vast tracts of land, like the Indus Valley Civilization.

Within a civilization you start thinking of others, through yajna—when you do something for others, and they do something for you in return. The long spoon used to put ghee in the yajna is called uddharini, which means to uplift and enable. The first line of the Rig Veda is about performing yajna with Agni in order to get ratna and dhatu—giving in order to get. Thus, the rishis and the rakshasas, both have culture, but only the rishis are considered civilized because only they practise yagna, or exchange, trade rather than raid. To be civilized, you have to connect with the other. Animals do not create culture. Humans create culture. But all cultures need not think of others. So they remain cultured, but not civilized.

Gold

The Ramayana abounds with references to gold—the golden Lanka, the golden deer, the golden statue of Sita, the golden plough with which Janaka finds the child, and the golden ornaments of Sita.

There is a golden lotus in the Mahabharata, too. One day, when Draupadi sees this golden lotus, she is filled with happiness. Bhima, one of the Pandavas, and one of her husbands, seeing this joy and her smile for the first time since her vastra-haran, decides to get the golden lotus for her.

References to gold are even found in the Vedas, like that of the Hiranyagarbha, or the golden womb.

In the Jatakas, too, there is a story of a swan whose feathers are made of gold. The swan gives one feather to each member of a family. But, in their greed, the family tries to capture the swan and take all the feathers by force. Thereon, the swan's feathers turn white again. This is the Indian version of the golden goose story. We also have the story of Parasmani, the philosopher's stone, where anything that touches it becomes gold.

Gold also populates Western myth. In the Bible, when Moses leads the Israelites out of Egypt to the Promised Land, there is the golden calf. The golden apple is important in Greek mythology. Eris, the goddess of quarrels, is incredibly mad because she wasn't invited to a wedding. So, she throws a golden apple with a note 'For the most beautiful woman' into the wedding. The three female goddesses present—Aphrodite, Hera, and Athena—fight to claim it. The gods, unable to give closure, tell them to reconcile this by going back to earth, to Paris, the prince of Troy, who will choose the most beautiful woman. Paris selects Aphrodite because she promises him Helen, truly the most beautiful woman, in return. Helen, who is actually married, gets kidnapped by Paris, and this sets off the infamous Trojan War. There's also the story of Midas where, like the Parasmani, everything he touches turns to gold.

But the question comes up: why is gold so popular?

It is malleable and ductile. It is a noble metal (resistant to chemical attack even at high temperatures) that doesn't get spoiled with time. It is thus a symbol of permanence that never rusts or blackens, and that is why it is associated with amrit, the nectar of immortality.

This concept of gold can be seen in Kashmiri Vaishnavism that became popular around the tenth century CE. The famous writer Abhinavagupta said the atma is like gold, it can take the form of an earring, a ring, a bracelet, a necklace, but at the end what remains is gold. Thus, gold is used to explain Advaita philosophy.

In India, before the arrival of the rishis there were the nagas, yakshas, and asuras, all three having some relation to gold. Nagas used to guard the gold, while the yakshas hired a mongoose to fight the naga and collect this gold treasure, turning yakshas into the lord of treasures. The asuras used to live underground, in Hiranyapura, the golden city, because gold is found underground. Hiranyayaksha, Hiranyakashipu, thus, are all asuras associated with gold.

I am reminded of a very interesting parable about Lakshmi. Lakshmi's sister, Alakshmi, came out of Halahala, the poison from the churning of the ocean. One day, both Lakshmi and Alakshmi confront a merchant, asking him which one of them is prettier. The merchant had to be careful, for he did not want to offend either of the goddesses. He cleverly replies, 'Lakshmi is prettier when coming towards me, and Alakshmi is prettier when she is moving away from me.' Thus he gets Lakshmi or fortune towards him and Alakshmi or misfortune away from him. This is why we keep sweets inside the house for Lakshmi during Diwali and lemons and chillies outside the house for Alakshmi. No one is rejected. But everyone is given a different place in the house.

Motherhood

We never look at our parents as human beings. Would you become friends with your parents if you met them at a party? What are their fears, ambitions, and traumas? There is an incomplete characterization, especially of mothers, that is also seen in our mythology.

A great example of this is Kaushalya, Rama's mother in the Ramayana. She is only seen as a mother, rarely a sister, a queen, a co-wife, or even a wife. We never see her loneliness, what her hobbies are, her likes and dislikes; her whole life revolves around giving birth to and agonizing over Rama.

In the Puranas, however, we begin to see the mother given different dimensions—vindictive, tired, unwilling, and unable to love. These traits are important, too, for if we don't see these aspects of mothers, with shades of ambivalence and cruelty, we get a sad one-dimensional caricature.

In the Padma Purana there is a famous story of Kansa's mother who is raped by a gandharva. When Kansa is born from that rape, she tells him that someone from the Yadava clan will kill him. There is hatred here between a mother and her son. Similarly, when Gandhari puts a cloth over her eyes in solidarity with her blind husband, Dhritarashtra, we don't talk about what this means for her children, the Kauravas—the psychological impact of having such parents, one who is unable to see them, and one who is unwilling to see them!

I am also interested in how Bharata's and Kaikeyi's relationship is affected when he comes back and realizes that, in her insecurity, she got Rama banished. Or with Menaka and Shakuntala—why was Shakuntala abandoned in childhood? This is when stories become not only interesting but multidimensional, giving the parents an interiority. This is why every year, on Mother's Day, I always say that it is important to not just celebrate their role but also make them human beings.

But, of course, not everyone has a mother. Someone once asked me who is the mother of Shiva and of Vishnu. Here, the concept of swayambhu becomes important—self-created and self-contained. Not taking birth *from* something.

Another distinction that I have spoken about before is between yonija and ayonija—the one born from the womb and not born from the womb. Rama and Krishna are born from the womb, so they will experience death, because those that experience birth must experience death. Examples of ayonija figures are Ganesha and Kartikeya—they are personified concepts and thus don't die. But, as exceptions, we have Sita, Draupadi, and the Buddha (in some retellings) as examples of ayonijas who experience death.

The Buddha's status is interesting because initially he was considered a yonija, but this changed later to ayonija or swayambhu through mythology. This was because slowly women started being seen as inferior, and thus marking someone an ayonija distances them from this inferiority. Women and the womb came to be associated with death. This is also why menstruation is also associated with death. Birth and death are both impure, a conceptual pollution that now begins to be attached to women.

In the Upanishads there is a famous story of Satyakama Jabala. When Gautama rishi asks him the name of his father, he says, 'I don't know. My mother is Jabala, who has had relations with many men and so she doesn't remember who my father is.' The guru is happy that he wasn't embarrassed by the truth, comfortable with it, and said it as it was.

In the Mahabharata, Kunti tells Pandu the story of Svetaketu, who belonged to a different age where women could have sexual relations with many people. But one day Svetaketu finds his mother with another man and gets very angry. For now he doesn't know who his real father could be. Thus, he created the rules of marriage, and from within it the idea of faithfulness and monogamy emerged.

Tale 52

Stages of Hinduism

Who discovered Hinduism?

Hinduism does not have figures like Jesus Christ and Prophet Muhammad. In the beginning, the Vedic religion was based on the idea of yajna or exchange. From this comes the idea of devta—a person who has something to offer. The concept of bhagwan comes much later. In some sense, everyone is a devta because everyone has something to offer—wealth or knowledge or power. This is why we fold our hands in prostration while doing namaste to everyone we see. It is a recognition of the devta in everyone.

Fire or agni is used during a yajna and, with this, the idea of tapasya comes to the fore. But tapas is about the psychological fire within. Yajna is the karma kanda of Hinduism, dealing with one's actions. Tapasya is known as the jnana kanda of Hinduism, dealing with one's knowledge. Jainism and Buddhism were born around this time, and they aligned with the idea of tapasya.

Yajna is about satisfying hunger. Tapasya is about destroying hunger, which is why in the Jain tradition fasting is so important.

From yajna to tapasya, Hinduism then begins to re-evaluate itself. Both are very masculine ideas. The female form is not important in either early Hinduism, Jainism, or Buddhism. The early stupas had no women, it was only when they made the railing around these structures that they included maithuna statues and images. One of the major differences between the ancient Theravada and the newer Mahayana Buddhist tradition, and the Jain Digambara and Svetambara traditions is how they see women. The rules for becoming a bhikkhuni (female bhikkhu) in the Vinaya Pitaka of Buddhism are a lot more in number than the rules to become a bhikkhu. It was often said that women needed to take another birth, and be reborn as men, to attain moksha.

In the third phase of Hinduism, women play an important role. There is an interesting story of how Mandana Mishra's wife, Ubhaya Bharati, asks Adi Shankara about Kama Shastra, but he says that since he has taken the vow of celibacy he cannot discuss this. At this point Ubhaya Bharati chastises him—how can one who cannot discuss sex, who hasn't experienced it, claim to have understood the whole world? Adi Shankara was educated by his mother. Now Ubhaya Bharati becomes his teacher.

Adi Shankara then goes to Kashmir where King Amaru is ailing. Adi Shankara, using Tantra, goes into his body, and through that body he learns the Kama Shastra, that Ubhaya Bharati chastised him for not knowing, and comes back to his own body. This story reveals how Hinduism slowly includes women and feminine power in its stories.

The concept of bhava, prem, and bhakti is thus

infused into Hinduism. Thus comes the Bhakti Kanda of Hinduism. This brings us back to yajna, where you have a reciprocal relationship with God, but this time, there is also love. Now, this is not cyclical. I would argue it is a spiral, because every time we come back to yajna, we are coming back to the same place, but we are also changed.

Tale 53

....

Ritual Stories

Indians have been telling stories for a long time. There is the Mahabharata, the Ramayana, the Puranas, the Agama stories, and the Jataka tales of the Buddha, and Sangam poetry. But there's also the *Katha Sarit Sagar,* the Panchatantra stories, Jain stories of the *Forest of Thieves,* Vikram and Vetal, *Dasa Kumar Charitram,* and *Singhasan Battisi.* Then you have folk tales of Birbal and Tenali Raman.

There are local epics like *Alha* in Bundelkhand, *Pabuji* in Rajasthan, *Ghoda and Maru, Lori and Chanda, Kedar–Gowri, Manasamangal Kavya, Shalivahan, Prithviraj Raso, Padmaavat,* Palnadi stories of Andhra Pradesh, *Sohni–Mahiwal,* Tapoi stories in Odisha, and *Satyanarayan.*

Later, when the Mughals came to India, the *Hamzanama* stories became very popular in the court. Since many rulers like Akbar were not literate, the royal karkhanas used to paint these stories for royal consumption. Sangam literature in the South produced mostly female-centric epics like *Manimekalai, Silappadikaram, Sukasaptati,* and even erotic stories.

One can ask: what is the significance of these stories and these traditions of storytelling? They could be either sacred tales, or parables to make one a better person, or they could serve as historical records, like diary entries, or they could just be a form of entertainment. Stories can also be told for specific moments. A vrat katha, for example, is a story to tell during pujas or vrat; it is an important part of the ritual.

The Tapoi stories, for example, are sung during the Khudurukuni Osha, where Mongala Ma is worshipped, in Odisha. The story is about seven brothers with their seven wives. The brothers have just one sister, Tapoi, who is much loved by everybody. When the brothers sail to Swarnadeep to do business, they are lost at sea. The sisters-in-law back home begin to treat Tapoi very badly. As she has no support, she prays to Mongala Ma, and her brothers return and her problems are solved. So you can see a structure developing—a happy beginning, a crisis, and a prayer to Devi to reverse the crisis. These are the vrat kathas of India through which deites are remembered and adored to bring their grace into our lives.

Tale 54

The Abandoned

There was a king called Harishchandra who had a health problem, an attack of dropsy where his body swelled up with fluid. He prayed to Varuna, god of water, and said, 'If I am cured, I will sacrifice my son.' As soon as he said this, he was cured, his fingers and face were no longer bloated. However, when Varuna asks him for the sacrifice, the king finds it hard to part with his son. So he calls the wise men of his kingdom, and tells them to find a way out of this problem, asking, 'How can I make Varuna happy without losing my son?'

The men come up with a plan. Since he has not mentioned which son he will sacrifice, he can adopt someone and then send that son for the sacrifice. Understandably, no one is willing to part with their child to have him sacrificed.

After a long search, the wise men find a poor priest, Ajigarta, who is willing to sell his son for 100 cows. He says, 'I have three sons. I will not sell my eldest son because he is very dear to me, and I cannot sell the youngest because he is dear to his mother. I will sell my middle son, Sunahshepa, because I have no choice. I am very poor and I need to feed my family.'

Thus, Sunahshepa is adopted by the king and brought to the palace on a golden palanquin. When, finally, the executioner is called to sacrifice the boy, he refuses because of guilt, 'I will not sacrifice the boy, he is no criminal.' Then, the butcher is called to sacrifice the boy, but he also refuses, 'I will not sacrifice the boy, he is no animal.'

Suddenly, a voice rings out across the sacrificial hall, 'I will! I will! For 100 more cows.' It was Ajigarta, Sunahshepa's own father! Everybody was aghast and looked at the father, and said, 'When you sold your son, your reason was poverty. What you're doing now sounds like greed.' The king, however, eager to please Varuna, accepted this exchange.

Watching his father move towards the chopping block, axe in hand, Sunahshepa realized he had no one to turn to. Both his father and his king, who were supposed to protect him, had abandoned him to death. In despair, he begs for divine intervention. Varuna, moved by the prayers, saves the boy. In some sense, it all ended well. But did it really?

Tale 55

Do You See Me?

Have you noticed how the pattern in the peacock feather looks like an eye? In Greek or Yavana mythology, when Zeus was frolicking with the nymphs, his wife Hera got very upset and sent Argus, a man with a hundred eyes to keep track of him, and to note if he was sleeping with other women. With his 100 eyes, at any given point of time, a pair of eyes was always open. This constant surveillance makes Zeus upset, and so he tells his son Hermes to play the harp and put Argus to sleep. When Argus goes to sleep, Hermes cuts his head off and Zeus continues his philandering. Hera is struck with grief at the death of Argus. In her grief, she takes the eyes of Argus and puts them on the tail of the peacock to memorialize him. This is why peacock feathers look like they have a hundred eyes pasted on them. They remind of the gods who can see what we try to hide.

There is a story of Surya's wife, Sanjana, who runs away from him. At first, in his self-absorption, he doesn't even notice that she has left him, mistaking her shadow, Chaya, which she left behind, for her. But when he finally notices, he gets angry, and goes to the divine craftsman, his father-in-law, Vishwakarma, demanding an explanation of why she left him. He tells Surya that in his brightness he made his wife invisible—instead of giving her light, he overshadowed her. This is exactly like many leaders and filmstars today, who are so self-obsessed that they see only themselves and no one else. Surya then dims his brightness, makes a sudarshana chakra from the light he gives away, and goes to his wife in the form of a horse. He learned his lesson, that a good relationship is about seeing the other and not just about being seen with them.

Tale 56

....

The Husband with Horns

Buffaloes and other horned animals are not considered evil in India. Harappan seals are full of horned men in yogic poses.

In village lore, we hear of the village goddess who kills her husband imagined as a buffalo. The buffalo's blood is mixed with seed and used in the field. He is killed only to be reborn with the next harvest. Thus sex and violence is intermingled in a village ritual. Sadly, this ritual is today misread as a battle of good over evil, with the buffalo being killed equated with a demon. In some stories, the husband is killed because he lies to the goddess. This justifies his killing. In other stories, he is not the husband but someone who has the audacity to be the husband of the goddess. But the older layers have no such moral arguments.

Look at this intermingling of sex and violence in nature. On a farm, you will notice among the many cows, there are only one or two stud bulls, meant to impregnate the cows. Similarly, in pig farms, a majority of the male pigs are castrated. We find the same in our myths; there is a very obvious privileging of only a few powerful men (rather like the stud bulls, or the pigs that are not castrated). This is true in nature because, from a reproductive angle, only a few men are needed. In Tantrik temples there are seven sisters or Saptamatrika and only one Bhairav.

The idea of a goddess who kills her old husband and marries a new husband, whose husbands dies and is reborn, is associated with the idea of women remarrying. There is a passage in the Rig Veda about how a widow used to go to the pyre of the husband and lie down beside him, only to be told to get up, by either a brother-in-law or second husband. So the widow enters the crematorium with one husband, and sometimes leaves with another. In the Ramayana, when Vali dies his widow Tara marries his brother Sugriva and when Ravana dies his widow Mandodari marries his brother Vibhishana.

Tale 57

Buddha's Topknot

In Shankaracharya's portraits, have you ever wondered why his head is covered? In the Buddha's iconography have you wondered about his topknot? Why is the Laughing Buddha bald?

In ancient times, being completely bald was thought to be inauspicious. Those who renounced the world completely would shave their heads. The Buddha does this when he leaves the palace. When a hunter saw the bald Buddha in the forest, he said to himself that today he won't be able to hunt any animal, since it is an inauspicious sight, and goes back home. This is why when the head is being shaved after a Hindu funeral, some hair is always left behind. He who completely renounces hair, renounces life.

Thus, as renunciants, Jain and Buddhist monks roamed around completely bald. The Buddha died around 500 BCE, but statues of him were made only about 500 years later. So, those who made sculptures of him never knew what he looked like. In earlier representations of the Buddha he was represented symbolically—a crown, or a plant, or his footprints were used as symbols to represent him without showing his face. With the arrival of the Greeks, the tradition of figurative sculpture began to take root. But they insisted on him having a head of hair, because baldness was considered inauspicious. So, they added the topknot. But this was at odds with the Buddhists who believed that being bald was a sign of renunciation. So an alternative explanation of this 'ushinisha' was given—that he has so much knowledge in his head, that there is a cranial protuberance. So, this is not a historical concept, but a mythological, even an artistic one!

Creatively, the people in Thailand use fire instead of the topknot. This is also the reason that Shankaracharya puts the cloth on his head, because he does not want to offend the sensibilities of the people. In medieval times, the head of widows was shaved if they refused to burn themselves on their husband's funeral pyre. They were kept in seclusion and considered impure and unlucky.

Now, in China and Japan, with Daoist and Shinto monks, there was nothing inauspicious associated with baldness, so the Laughing Buddha, found mostly in these areas, is often bald. Baldness was, in fact, considered a sign of beauty.

Gender Fluidity

When Rama finishes his education with Vasistha he says he wants to become a tapasvi, or hermit, not a raja, or king. Then Vasistha speaks to him through beautiful stories compiled in the book *Yoga Vaishtha*, and then Rama decides to not become a tapasvi, but a tapasvi-raja.

One of the stories Vasistha tells Rama is the story of Chudala. Chudala is a queen but also a tapasvini. Her husband, the king, also wants to become a tapasvi. The queen offers the king her services, saying she could teach him all he needs to know when he is free between his royal duties. But he dismisses her, insisting that his guru be male. He then decides to go to the forest in pursuit of this male guru. Chudala manages the royal affairs while her husband tries in vain to acquire self-knowledge in the forest. Chudala, trying to take things into her hands, changes form, becomes a man, Kumbaka, and flies to the forest to teach her husband all he wants to know. Her husband now listens to Kumbaka, and learns from him. One day, to test her husband to see if he is ready to become a tapasvi-raja, Chudala devises three tests.

(Chudala as) Kumbaka tells him that he is cursed to turn into a woman, Madanika, at night. As night falls, Madanika asks the king if he will have sex with her. The king declares that he will be the bhog but not the bhogi, which means that even if he is not hungry, he will allow Madanika's hunger to be satisfied. So, Madanika satisfies herself, while he finds no need to satisfy himself. (The test of moh.)

The next day Madanika tells him that she wants to have sex with someone else, and the king doesn't mind this. There was no anger, or attachment to her. (The test of krodh.)

On the third day when Indra comes and asks him to come to heaven with him, he refuses, saying that heaven is in the mind. (The test of lobh.)

Seeing this, Kumbaka is thrilled and turns back into the queen. She tells her husband that he can now come back to the palace and become tapasvi-raja, the ideal king he always wanted to be, for he doesn't have moh, krodh, or lobh.

Now this story talks of detached kingship through a tale of gender fluidity. Here, we have a king who sees this man turning into a woman and doesn't mind having sex with her, which means he has no issues with fluid sexuality.

There is even a story in the Baul tradition where Kali is standing on top of Shiva. Kali then turns into Krishna, and so Shiva, in response, turns into Radha. Again, gender and sexuality becomes fluid. This is our heritage.

Across India, you will find temples where the god and goddess are placed side by side. But there are many devi temples where you find two goddesses side by side. In

North India, there is Nanda–Sunanda, in the South there is Sammakka–Saralamma, in Odisha there is Tar–Tarini, in Gujarat there is Chamunda–Chotila. Some people say these pairs are sisters, or mothers and daughters, and some say they are sakhis, female companions who go to war together. This shows a world where a woman doesn't need a man to be seen as a complete figure. This also shows that people did live in communities or communes of single-sex companionship, like the Saptarishi, or the Saptamatrika, or the Navanath. Not everything was seen through a heteronormative lens. All kinds of communities and families were imagined.

Tale 59

Numbers

India is the country that discovered the two most important numbers in maths and science—zero or shunya, and infinity or ananta; nothingness and completeness.

Infinity can be scary. To control this uncontrollable uncertainty, we use numbers, and algorithms. If I ask you how much work you have done today, you might find it hard to answer me concretely. But if I ask, tell me three things you did today, I have given the question structure, and it is easier to answer. Numbers help organize knowledge.

Numbers also help us remember things. The Gita has eighteen chapters. The Mahabharata also has eighteen chapters; it climaxes in a battle involving eighteen armies. If you notice, so many of our festivals have numeric names: Ashtami, Navami, Dashami, Ekadashi, Dwadashi, Trayodashi, Dhanteras, Navratri.

This isn't just limited to Hinduism, Buddhism, and Jainism. Think of the twelve Apostles of Jesus Christ, the importance of seven in the Bible (seven days to create the world) or the seventy-two Houris from the Hadith. There is even the famous Friday the thirteenth when the Knights Templar, celibate Catholic warriors, also bankers, were massacred by King Philip IV.

Let us look at some popular use of numbers in Hindu mythology.

One	▪ Ekapada: the form of Shiva who stands on one foot.
Two	▪ Dvaita philosophy: the belief that the atman and the brahman are distinct, propounded by Madhvacharya. ▪ The two heads of Agni.
Three	▪ Tri-kala: past, present, or future. ▪ Tri-guna: tamas, satva, rajas. ▪ Tri-lok: swarg, dharti, pataal. ▪ Tri-dev: Brahma, Vishnu, Maheswara. ▪ Trinetra: the three eyes of Shiva.
Four	▪ Chaturveda: the four Vedas. ▪ Chaturmukh: the four faces of Brahma. ▪ The four animals of the Mauryan symbol: lion, elephant, horse, bull.
Five	▪ The Panch Pandavas. ▪ Five Karmendriya or Action Organs: hands, legs, mouth, genitals, and anus. ▪ Five Gyanendriya or Sense Organs: eye, ear, nose, tongue, skin.
Six	▪ Sashti: six seasons.
Seven	▪ Sapta Sindhu or seven rivers. ▪ Saptarishi: Agastya, Atri, Bhardwaja, Gautam, Jamadagni, Vasistha, and Vishvamitra. (According to the Jaiminiya Brahmana). ▪ Saptha Kanya. ▪ Sapta Sur: Sa, Re (Ri in Carnatic), Ga, Ma, Pa, Dha, Ni.
Eight	▪ Ashtadhatu: literally means eight metals. These are alloys. ▪ Ashta Lakshmi: eight forms of wealth. ▪ Ashta Bhairav: eight forms of Shiva located in cardinal and ordinal directions. ▪ Ashta Siddhi: eight supernatural powers of yogis.

Nine	■ Nava Dwaarpura: the body is compared with a city with nine gates—two eyes, two ears, two nostrils, one mouth, one anus, and one genital opening. ■ Navagraha: Surya (Sun), Chandra (Moon), Mangala (Mars), Budha (Mercury), Brihaspati (Jupiter), Shukra (Venus), Shani (Saturn), Rahu (eclipse creator), Ketu (comet).
Ten	■ Ten directions: four cardinal directions, four ordinal directions, up and down.
Eleven	■ Indra attacks the womb of Aditi, which he fears will kill him, with a vajra, dividing the foetus in her womb into eleven parts. These eleven children start to cry, so their mother says 'Ma Ruda', meaning 'Don't cry'. That's how the name Maruta comes about. Shiva and Vayu, the wind-god, are connected with them.
Sixteen	■ Solah shringar. ■ When Adi Shankara goes to Kashi he is said to have met Vyasa who told him, at age eight, that if he wants to live for eight more years, he must learn the Vedas, which he does and lives to sixteen. At this point Vyasa tells him that if he wants to live for sixteen more years, he must travel and spread the word of the Vedas, which he does till he dies at the age of thirty-two.
Thirty-two and Sixty-four	■ Thirty-two gunas or qualities that make Buddha. ■ Singhasan Battisi: The thirty-two qualities to become a king. Double it to get sixty-four which are the qualities to become a courtesan. Thirty-two qualities to be a king, sixty-four for a courtesan. Isn't that interesting? ■ This thirty-two concept comes perhaps from thirty-two teeth.
Thirty-three	■ Thirty-three gods of Vedic and Buddhist mythology: twelve Adityas, eight Vasus, eleven Maruts, two Ashvins.
Fifty-six	■ Chappan Bhog: eight bhogs per day x seven days a week = fifty-six bhogs.

Sixty-three	▪ Mahapurusha of Jains: nine triads of Vasudeva-Baladeva-Prativasudeva + twenty-four tirthankaras + twelve chakravartis = sixty-three. ▪ Sixty-three Nayanar saints of the South: Nayanars are Shaiva bhakts. The Shaivas were perhaps influenced by Jains who were also their rivals in ancient Tamilakkam.
Hundred, Thousand	▪ 1,000 names of Vishnu. ▪ 1,000 eyes of Varuna. ▪ 100 eyes of Indra.

Tale 60

The Granaries of Yusuf

As per Islamic lore, Idris used to live in Babylon trying to convince people of the greatness of Allah. But no one would listen to him. In anger, he began travelling until he reached the shores of the river Nile in Egypt (or Misr-desh), where he gasped at the crystal blue beauty of the river. He exclaimed words used for the first time, 'Subhan Allah', amazing in the name of god. It is believed that Idris started the Egyptian Civilization. Of course, now religious figures in the country are saying that Idris also built the pyramids. Archaeologists and historians vehemently disagree with this, because the pyramids predate Islam by 3,000 years.

The Prophet Abraham (Ibrahim, in Arabic), like Idris believed in one God, not many gods.

Ibrahim's great grandson, Yusuf, was known as a dream-interpreter and the most beautiful man. For a long time people referred to the pyramids of Egypt as the Granaries of Yusuf—a reference to him becoming the second-in-command of the pharaoh, helping manage the grain of Egypt produced in seven years of prosperity to tide over seven years of famine.

It was only in the nineteenth century that we found out that the pyramids were actually the tombs of kings, built when the Harappan Civilization reached its mature phase (2500 BCE).

The Stories We Tell

This is thus the story of how Ibrahim's children came to Egypt and built a civilization whose marker still stands to this day. Later, Musa or Moses would take them out of Egypt because the king treated them badly, but that is another story.

Tale 61

....

Horses

The earliest images we have of horses come from the following places:

1. The Hyksos of Western Asia, in 1500 BCE, when they settled along the river Nile.

2. The Mitani inscriptions in Turkey in 1300 BCE. In their horse training manuals, we find the mention of the Vedic gods Indra and Varuna.

3. Egyptian battles with the Hittites in 1200 BCE.

Around this time, the Rig Veda was being composed in India where horses are the most important animal. The Vedic gods—Indra, Varuna, Agni, all ride on raths or chariots pulled by horses, a new invention of that time. Horses, we now know from ancient DNA studies, were domesticated only in 2000 BCE near the Black Sea. They spread towards Europe, Egypt, and India five centuries later.

Even in Buddhism, which emerges later, when the Buddha first goes around the city as a prince, he is on a chariot. When he leaves the city to take up sanyas, he leaves on horseback. From Norse mythology's Sleipnir, the horse with eight legs, to Pegasus, the winged horse from Greek mythology, horses clearly have a pride of place in later mythologies.

The Asvamedha Yajna, when a horse is sent across territories with a message of the king's dominion, becomes a way to spread territorial reach. The Avesta of Iran written around the same time, too, uses horses as an integral part of its culture.

By 1300 BCE, the Aryans reached the Northern Gangetic plains. In the Ramayana the rath is important— Rama leaves Ayodhya on a horse-drawn chariot. The same motif is in the Bhagavat Purana, of Krishna leaving Gokul on a chariot, and the gopis mourning. Krishna also propounds the Bhagavad Gita from a rath. In the manthan, the churning of the ocean, one of the fourteen elements to come out is a horse!

While horses and chariots existed, the riding of horses, however, came much later, during the Greek and Persian period with Alexander. It was a period when Indians would buy horses from Central Asia and sell elephants. Thus Indian kings were called Gajapatia and the kings of the Northwest were called Ashvapathia (Kaikeyi's father too was an Ashvapathi). The oldest image of a horse in India is found in a Buddhist cave in Sanchi. On the chariot of the sun-god are female archers shooting arrows. You also find these chariots of the sun in the Bhaja caves near Pune.

Thus, with the Greeks, horse riding enters the Indian imagination. The literature produced around this time reflects this. Indra's son, Jayant, and Surya's son, Revant, are imagined as riding horses, and hunting. The concept of Kalkin, the tenth avatara of Vishnu, riding a horse, too, comes around this time. Kalkin's first mention in the Puranas is around 400 CE. The Navagraha became popular roughly 1,000 years ago. Among the Navagrahas, Brihaspati (Jupiter) is associated with elephants, and Shukracharya (Venus) is associated with horses.

Local deities riding horses like Khandoba, Momaji, Mallanna Veer Tejaji, and the Rajput divinities too come about slowly and steadily. Even to this day, terracotta horses are given as offerings to the village warrior and guardian gods. In Gujarat, there is a temple of seventy-two horsemen. In the Durga temples in the South, you will notice a horse rider, Muttal Ravuttan, the server of Durga. Hayagriva, the horse-headed Vishnu, is famous in South India. Vedic knowledge was given by Vishnu to mankind through him—the kudre-mukh or horse mouth.

There is a very famous fight known in Odisha between the king of Kanchi and the king of Puri. Kanchi's king was giving his daughter to the king of Puri. But when he comes, he sees the king sweeping his own chariots with a broom. Thus dismissing him as a low-caste king he walks away. In anger, Puri's king goes towards Kanchi to prove that God is with him. On the way he meets a woman selling curd who tells him that before him two men passed by. A dark man (Krishna) who was riding a white horse, and a fair man (Balarama) riding a dark horse. They both bought curd and told her the king of Puri would pay for it. The king of Puri realizes that he has the support of the gods as he goes to battle the king of Kanchi.

There is another interesting story regarding the Ashwini Kumars (also known as Ashvins) who are seen as having the head of a horse. (Centaurs in Greek mythology have the hindquarters of a horse.) The Ashvins wanted Rishi Dadichi to give them Soma Yajna (knowledge). But they knew Indra was against this. Indra had told Dadichi that his head would explode if he shared the secret. The Ashvins decided on a plan. They cut off the head of Dadichi and replaced it with a horse head that could give them the knowledge. When the horse head exploded, they replace it with Dadichi's original head. In another story, Yagnavalkya gets knowledge of the Vedas from the sun-god who takes the form of a horse. Thus, the horse is linked not just to the arrival of Aryans but to Vedic knowledge.

Infidelity

There are three stories dealing with infidelity in the Ramayana:

1. Jamadagni–Renuka

2. Gautam–Ahalya

3. Rama–Sita

In all these three stories, the female character is related to the earth or fertility. Renu means pollen, but also sand. Ahalya means fallow land. Sita means furrow.

Renuka lusts briefly for a man she has just seen. This is considered emotional or psychological infidelity. For this, her husband, Jamadagni, asks for her head to be cut off.

Ahalya is said to have slept with Indra. Depending on the version of the story you prefer, she either did not know he was Indra, and was tricked into sleeping with him, or was voluntarily there. Here, it is physical infidelity. Ahalya is made into a rock or made invisible as a form of punishment.

Sita's supposed infidelity is only through hearsay. It is neither physical nor psychological. It is an alleged stain on royal reputation.

These three stories come from this idea that women

have to be faithful to men. No one asks men to be faithful. Rama is the only character in Hindu mythology who is described as ekam-patni-vrata, faithful to a single wife.

Now, we all know about the *Kama Sutra*. But few would have heard about the *Ananga Ranga*, a text written for married people. The story goes that a woman enters the king's court naked, asking the king how she is supposed to remain faithful when her husband doesn't give her pleasure. She asks if anyone at the court can write an erotic manual that will help satisfy her. *Ananga Ranga* was thus written. Here, the responsibility of the wife's fidelity rests with the husband and his ability to make her happy.

With all this in mind, it perhaps makes sense why people say the Mahabharata should not be read in your house. It is full of demanding female characters, which people are afraid of. Most men prefer Sita from the Ramayana who is mostly docile, easy to control, and accuse, even without a morsel of evidence.

Look at the tale of Savitri from the Mahabharata, a woman so well-read that everyone around her would tell her parents that she would never get married. Her father tells her to marry whomever she wishes to. So, she goes on to marry Satyavan. But her parents find out that according to Satyavan's horoscope he will die within a year. Savitri remains unperturbed by this, unafraid of even Yama, the god of death. When Yama finally comes to take her husband, Savitri follows him persistently. Yama finally gets irritated by this, and gives her three boons to let him be; the only thing she could not ask for was her husband's life.

The following were her wishes:

1. My father-in-law's kingdom should be returned.

2. My father must be given a son.

3. I want a child with Satyavan.

Yama was impressed that she first asked for a boon for others, and then herself. This is an indicator of compassion born of wisdom. Savitri brushes this aside and asks, 'How can I become the mother of Satyavan's son unless he is brought back to life?' to which Yama laughs, realizing her wit in the face of grief, and Satyavan is brought back to life.

The point of this story is that here we have a woman saving a man's life. There are other similar stories such as that of Nala–Damayanti. Draupadi, too, makes sure that the Pandavas get their property back. The wife rescues the husband in these stories from the Mahabharata.

The Stories We Tell

Tale 63

The East India Company and Hinduism

This whole idea of 'defending Hinduism' comes from the British.

Raja Rammohun Roy, in 1816, was the first person to use the word 'Hinduism'. The early 1800s was the age of reform with Roy's Brahmo Samaj and much later the Arya Samaj trying to erase archaic traditions like sati, child marriage, and encourage widow remarriage. But there was a backlash by people who feared that Hinduism was becoming too anglicized, and accommodating for the British. So, in 1894, Chandranath Basu came up with the idea of 'Hindutva', which is a word in common parlance today.

Hinduism comes from a reformer; Hindutva comes from a traditionalist who believes Hinduism does not require change. V. D. Savarkar in the early twentieth century starts using 'Hindutva' differently, as a political ideology, where India belongs only to those who see India as a holy land or punya-bhoomi and the land of their ancestors or pitrabhoomi. That would exclude Christians and Muslims, would it not?

But what if we take this thread a little back, and ask: what did people call themselves before 1816? Was there a name for a unified religion called Hinduism?

In the works of Chaitanya Mahaprabhu, Kabir, and

even the works produced during the Vijayanagara empire of the fourteenth century, 'Hindu Dharma' was used to distinguish local Indian culture from the new culture that was coming with the Turks, identified as Turuka Dharma. The difference was cultural. The idea of religion as a category emerged only in the nineteenth century around the world because of European colonizers.

When the East India Company, new rulers of India, lost the war against the Afghans in 1842, they were asked why they took Indians all the way to Afghanistan to fight this war. The Company had a ready reply—that they wanted to get the doors of Somnath back, and to save Hindus from Muslims who had ruled over them for centuries. The seeds of bigotry and communal divide were sown at that moment. The doors that were brought back from Ghazni turned out to have no connection with Somnath.

Then, when the Company translated the Vedas, and discovered the similarity between Sanskrit and Latin, their narrative changed. The idea of the Aryan language originating in India got significant traction. They began to say, 'Both of us come from the same lands, so in a sense, we are not invaders, we are all Aryans, and the British are back in India, the original homeland.' This idea appealed to many elite Hindus. Thus the English had made themselves brothers of Hindus and they both had a common enemy—the Muslim rulers of the land, the nawabs, the nizams, and the sultans.

Then, around the First War of Independence in 1857,

the linguistic journey of Sanskrit began to be studied more deeply. It was found that Sanskrit, like Hinduism, comes from outside India, from the steppes of Eurasia. This suggested (rather conveniently) that not just the British but also the Sanskrit-speaking Brahmins were of foreign origin. This upset the Brahmins who had insisted both Muslims and the English were foreigners. And, with this, you can see how the British story vis-a-vis Hinduism kept changing depending on the vested interests they had and the research available at that time. First the Muslims were outsiders, then the British were distant European cousins of Brahmins, and eventually even Brahmins were outsiders.

This constant need to unite and divide society on the basis of religion is a British construct. But societies are extremely complicated. Everyone seems to talk about the destruction of Somnath as a sign of declining Hinduism, and thus build this narrative of reviving Hinduism. But did you know, in Odisha, the Jagannath Temple was attacked twenty-three times? But we are still worshipping in it today. Madurai was attacked so many times, it still survived. So, things have a way of surviving. And if they don't, perhaps they weren't meant to endure. And that's okay. Time and geography change things. Indian philosophy teaches us impermanence. What goes up, comes down and what comes down, goes up. Eventually.

Tale 64

Board Games

Chess or shatranj, like so many modern board games—ludo and snakes and ladders—was invented in India, and from here it travelled to Persia, Arabia, and finally Europe. It is said that snakes and ladders was invented by the Jains, as a karma-patta, to represent karma—the snakes representing bad karma and the ladders representing good karma. Then, there's also chausar, cowrie shells, ganjifa cards, and dice-based games.

The earliest dice in the world was, in fact, found in Harappa. Remember the dice referenced in the Mahabharata? It was made from Shakuni's father's bones so it could roll in any direction that Shakuni decided. That is why Yudhishthira lost everything.

There is also an intriguing story of Karna playing dice with Duryodhana's wife, Bhanumati. When Duryodhana enters the room, Bhanumati feels awkward, and decides to leave. But Karna extends his hands to her saying she can't leave. When he pulls at her necklace it breaks. People always use this as evidence of Karna having an affair with her. But Duryodhana trusted Karna wholeheartedly, saying that Karna treats his wife as his sister. This is why Karna decided to remain with Duryodhana, who had great faith in him, despite Krishna's advise that he should support the Pandavas. How do you turn your back on someone who believes in you, even if they make wrong, unfair decisions and choose war over peace, clinginess over sharing?

Note how most games we play today are competitive. Our victory is almost always about someone else's loss. When Krishna is playing with his friends in Gokul, the Raslila and Dahi Handi are all collaborative. But when he enters the Mahabharata it is all competitive—dice and war.

We often teach competition, never collaboration. What is the allure of competition? Of gambling? I think more than the dopamine rush, it is the high of triumphing over others that makes us keep playing against one another. With gambling, it is the fear of coming to the edge and surviving. When you compete it is an adrenaline rush, when you collaborate it is a serotonin rush. Perhaps as a civilization, we are growing to prefer the former.

Expiry Dates

Cronus is the name of a Greek god of time, from where the word 'chronology' comes. Time eats everything. There is a popular story of Cronus eating his own children because he found out that one of his children would kill him.

Cronus' wife, Rhea, fed up with her husband eating all her children, places a rock in her cradle to fool her husband while raising her newborn secretly in a cave. The child grows up to eventually kill his father. This idea of a younger generation murdering the older generation is a metaphor for the churn of culture. This moral rings more presciently today, especially in regard to the way old politicians keep holding onto power keeping the younger, more energetic, and idealistic politicians out of power; rather like Bhishma, till the very end of the Mahabharata, in the Shanti Parva, not sharing knowledge with the next generation; this is also reminiscent of the older actors in Bollywood.

It was to prevent this from happening that the ashrama concept was built into Hindu culture. So, after one point you must retire from productive life, and leave for the forest, making way for the next generation.

This idea of being forever young and immortal is thus counter to the idea of ashrama where everything has an expiry date.

This is why there are no permanent structures in the Vedic age. The whole structure of a yajna is supposed to be burned down once used; there should not be any trace of it. The same idea is found in the festivals of Ganesha and Durga where images of the deity are created, worshipped but eventually dissolved in water. Rituals thus reinforce the idea of impermanence.

The Jains tell a story of how Baladeva, weeping copiously when Vasudeva dies, keeps trying to feed the dead body. A rishi comes by, places a rock on the ground and feeds it water, and this baffles everyone who asks him what he is trying to do. He says he wants the rock to birth a lotus and people laugh at him. The rishi says that if a lotus cannot bloom from this rock, why do you hope a dead body can become alive again? Baladeva realizes the futility of expecting the dead to come back to life.

A yaksha once asked Yudhishthira, 'What is the most unique thing about this world?'

Yudhishthira answered, 'Every day people die, and the rest of us live as if we are immortal.'

....

From the Middle East to India

Let us first visualize the Middle East geographically. In the extreme west is Turkey, and on the eastern end is Persia (Iran), and in between we have Mesopotamia (Iraq), Arabia (Saudi Arabia), Misr-desh (Egypt), and the Levant (Israel).

This was the land of the Sumerians, Akkadians, Elamites, Eblaites, and Babylonians. The civilization here, housed between the rivers Tigris and Euphrates (in modern day Iraq), was fertile ground to make bricks, and to farm. The ziggurat is the most famous structure of this time, made from sun-baked bricks. It was multistoreyed so that the priests could take refuge here during floods. You can see how the image of big floods and the precautions taken against it will later fuel stories like that of Noah's Ark.

The cuneiform script, the oldest in the world, also comes from here. People here believed that the gods made humans to serve them, creating a servant–master relationship. Diagonally opposite we have Egypt, where we find the concept of king, monarchy, and empire emerging. If Mesopotamia had many gods and many kings then Egypt had many gods but only one main king.

The Jewish Torah (the Old Testament) originated in the Levant, and by virtue of its geography is thus influenced by both Mesopotamia in the east and Egypt in the south. Stories of God creating the world in seven days, of Genesis, of the Garden of Eden, of Adam and Eve are told. From these stories we can conclude that obedience becomes the key feature of a believer. The idea that there is a wrathful God to bow down to in servility takes root. While Egypt has one king with many gods and Mesopotamia has many gods with many kings, Levant, also known as Canaan, speaks of one all-powerful God, spelt with capitals and in singular, who will have only one king.

Saul, David, and Solomon are kings who rule this region of Israel, but slowly they move towards polytheism, and idol worship. When the Babylonians and Assyrians conquered Israel, they forcibly relocated the educated and powerful Jews to Persia. Now, in Persia a new idea of monotheism—of one good, kind God—comes about under Zoroastrianism; the idea of a noble king associated with this noble God, who will do good for his public, solidifies the idea of empire. The division between good and bad becomes clear and strong. All bad deeds come from Angra Mainyu (the Zoroastrian Devil) while all good deeds spring forth from Ahura Mazda (the Zoroastrian God).

Then, 2,000 years ago, near Jerusalem in Israel, a carpenter, Isa or Jesus, said that God is love and forgiveness. God is not meant to be feared. He not only calls himself the messenger but also the 'Son of God', and calls attention to how his sacrifice will forgive all humans, thus bringing the idea of a saviour front-and-centre. Christianity was then a small religion.

Then, less than 1,700 years ago, when the Roman empire becomes Christian, the world changes. Religion becomes political. Unlike the old Roman empire, Christian Rome does not tolerate other religious practices. When the Barbarians attack Rome, and the king takes refuge in Byzantium (Istanbul), the Church splits—we now have a Roman Church and a Byzantium Church. Note that Islam has not yet arrived on the scene.

Around 600 CE, a man called Muhammad emerges, and he is identified as a 'Messenger of God'. In Mecca—a pilgrim site where they pray to idols—no one believes him, and he is forced to leave and go to Medina. This journey is known as the Hijr, or separation. In Medina, he emerges as a military leader who comes back to defeat Mecca, thus removing all other religions practised there. This reflects in the Quran too, where the verses composed in Mecca are more spiritual, and the ones in Medina are more political. Monotheism now dominates the Middle East.

What was happening in India during the seventh century when Islam was rising in the Middle East?

Harshavardhana was ruling in the North. Hiuen Tsang was visiting India. In the South, the Pallavas were building stone temples, enshrining Mahishasura Mardhini, and Vishnu. The Ellora caves were carved with images of Tara holding a lotus, symbolic of Mahayana Buddhism. Tara is seen as a mixture of Saraswati and Durga.

After the Prophet dies, his followers establish the Caliphate and suddenly transform Islam into a formidable military force, destroying the Byzantine and Zoroastrian empires. Within 200 years, this whole region comes under their control, from Persia to Spain. The Mediterranean region splits into Christian Europe and Muslim Africa. The Crusades, a series of religious wars of the tenth century, ensue.

Note that this is a broad brushstroke story because religion is not a monolith. The Islam of Arabia is very different from that in Turkey which is different from that in Persia which is different from that in Indonesia. For example, the early Arab Muslims would allow Christian pilgrims to travel. But when the Seljuk Turks came along, they did not allow the Christians to travel for pilgrimage and this is why the Crusades began.

Then, in the twelfth century, Islam enters India with Mohammad Ghuri. The Mamluk or slave dynasty ends up ruling India, setting up the Delhi Sultanate and later, in the sixteenth century, Babur sets up the Mughal empire. The Turkic kings were not attached to land and they did not believe in the hierarchy of caste. So they were not rooted to a land or a village, they could travel anywhere seeking fortune. In the thirteenth century, Mongols destroyed the city of Baghdad and refugees poured into India bringing Persian culture to the Gangetic plains.

By the sixteenth century, India was controlled by the Mughals, Persia by the Safavids, and Turkey by the Ottomans. The whole belt was under Muslim kings, much as, a millennium earlier, the region from Afghanistan to Thailand was ruled by Hindu kings, called the 'Sanskrit Cosmopolis'. In seventeenth-century Bengal, there was a writer called Sayyed Sultan who translated Islamic lore into Bengali, *Nabi Bonsa,* which means the lineage of prophets. In South India, we find the *Seerapuranam* in Tamil, on the life of Prophet Muhammad. Mappila poetry about the Prophet's marriage is, even today, recited during weddings.

The Muslims' control of the Silk and Spice Routes led to the European Dark Ages when they could no longer depend on trade for development. But soon, the European Enlightenment comes about and the world is forced to reorganize again—with that comes colonialism, then industrialization. The world keeps churning.

Tale 67

....

Lakshmana's Sleep

Urmila is Lakshmana's wife. Stories of her come mostly from folk tales. During the fourteen-year vanvaas when Lakshmana accompanied Rama and Sita in exile, he did not sleep a wink. At night, he watched over Rama and Sita as they slept, and during the day, he stood beside them to protect them from the creatures of the forest. When Nidra Devi, the goddess of sleep, came to him, Lakshmana told her to give his share of sleep to his wife so he may continue performing his brotherly duties. So, he outsources sleep and Urmila sleeps for fourteen years. This becomes important to defeat Indrajit, Ravana's son, because Indrajit is told that only a person who never sleeps could kill him.

In Andhra Pradesh, this story is taken further—that during Rama's coronation Nidra Devi comes to deliver the fourteen years of sleep that Lakshmana has done without. Lakshmana laughs at the irony of the situation because the one thing he wanted to see was Rama's coronation, and now he won't be able to do so because he will be in deep sleep. There is a long poem in Telugu on this laughter, because Bharata thinks Lakshmana is laughing at him, Kaikeyi thinks he is laughing at her, and so on. Everyone in the kingdom thinks they are being laughed at by Lakshmana. This story is interesting in another sense. Rama has a brother who never sleeps, while Ravana has a brother who always sleeps, Kumbhakarna. What are the odds that this was a consciously designed narrative trope used by Rishi Valmiki, to tell us the difference between a good king and a bad king?

....

How Abrahamic Faiths Differ

The story of Jesus Christ comes from the four Gospels of Matthew, Mark, Luke, and John in the Bible's New Testament, written in Greek within a century of Jesus's death.

Before Christianity, we had the Jewish people who believed in Yahweh. The Romans who were then ruling Jerusalem did not care for gods and goddesses. They only believed in the empire. In a way, this is secular—equal disdain for all religions.

In the midst of the Roman empire, suddenly, a narrative comes out of a person who is crucified. It is said that three days later he disappeared from his grave and was born again, resurrected. His twelve Apostles travel all over the world to spread the word that God has sacrificed his son for the benefit of humanity. This was a new story! Before this, the stories were about Yahweh, a God who must be feared and whose rules must be adhered to. Now, it was about a kind God loving you. The all-powerful God emerging from the Middle East transforms from one who demands obedience to one who forgives. From Jerusalem this story goes to Rome and Greece. By 300 CE, this becomes the most powerful story in the Middle East.

Christians believe that the Jewish traditions of the Old Testament were the seed from which Christianity emerged. But where they diverge is with Christ. Jews don't believe that the Messiah has taken a human form on earth. Christians do—his name is Jesus Christ or Isa. In Islam, however, Isa is not considered the son of God, he is simply a messenger, the one who came before Prophet Muhammad. He is also not crucified in their telling of his tale. Isa is mentioned as the one who will triumph over the Devil on the Day of Deliverance.

See how the three Abrahamic religions—Judaism, Christianity, and Islam—though springing from the same area with a similar cast of characters can be so different. The Christians have often treated the Jews badly. The Jews have often treated the Muslims badly. The Muslims and the Christians have often fought; one of their points of contention, for example, had to do with their views on marriage and celibacy—Jesus was unmarried, whereas Prophet Muhammad was married more than once. On occasion, this led to conflict between conservative Christian traditions of celibacy and Islamic ideas of marriage.

One point of convergence was the attitude towards music and dance. Both Islam and Christianity don't like dance in the religious context. The Christians, however, allowed hymns and singing in the church, which is forbidden in mosques. Dance is permitted in a secular context, as in ballroom dance or ballet but this is a remnant of folk traditions and later court culture. The church in the Dark Ages, before Reformation, frowned upon any display of the body, much like Wahhabi Islam today. The Hagia Sophia of Istanbul, which was a great church famous for its music, today, converted into a mosque, has no music playing in it. Such are the vagaries of time.

Tale 69

....

Ardhanareshwara

In Ardhanareshwara, the half-woman form of Shiva, for the first time we are seeing the male and female being given equal importance, in one body, beating with the same heart.

But take note that when we speak of Ardhanareshwara, we always talk about this god as a form of Shiva, and never that of Shakti. Shiva here is half a woman. Shakti is never called half a man. The reason for this is unclear. But Shiva's association with Shakti is an obvious challenge to the then reigning Buddhist tradition. If you notice, as the Buddha leaves his householder life to become an ascetic figure, we have Shiva, an ascetic figure, brought down from the mountains, and made a householder—he is making the opposite journey. He becomes Shankara and his marriage with Shakti (or Parvati) crystallizes in the form of Ardhanareshwara.

The Nataraja statue that is so common today has a defining characteristic that helps differentiate between Shiva, the ascetic, and Shankara, the householder. In the statue, the left leg is usually in the air, and the right leg is firmly planted on the ground. The left leg suspended mid-air is a sign of sanyas. In the Meenakshi temple in Madurai, however, you will find Shiva's right leg is in the air, his left leg planted squarely on the ground.

This is because here Shiva is the householder, married to Meenakshi Amma. If you look carefully at a Nataraja statue, he has male earrings on the right side and female earrings on the left side, once again reminding us that he includes the feminine, unlike the ascetic community of India. To marry or not to marry, to include or exclude the feminine, to be hermit or householder, is a recurring theme of Indian lore.

Tale 70

....

Emotional Infidelity

The story of Renuka Devi, a goddess worshipped in southern Maharashtra and northern Karnataka, outlines her loyalty as the wife of Rishi Jamadagni. One day, at the river, she sees a handsome man and for a moment is enamoured, housing some affection, bordering on lust. The rishi finds out about this furtive moment of lust in her thoughts and is deeply angered by it. He asks his sons to cut off her head as punishment. Four of the sons refuse to cut off their mother's head, and thus, are made napunsaka, or castrated eunuchs. However, the youngest son, Parashurama, willingly cuts off the mother's head, and his father grants him a boon for following his orders. Intelligently, he asks for his mother to be brought back to life. The rishi agrees, and tells him to go to a certain spot, spill some water there, and walk back, without looking back to see if his mother is brought back to life. After spilling the water he walks back home, but dire curiosity takes over and he ends up looking back. At that point only his mother's face was formed, and so even to this day only the head of Renuka Devi is worshipped.

There is another Maharashtrian story, that of Jambul Akhiyan. Jambul is the jamun fruit, called the Indian blackberry, that can be found growing at the height of summer. (Incidentally, India is called Jambudweep because the jamun grows here.) When you eat the fruit, your mouth is dyed a deep purple. The story goes that one day Draupadi, despite having five husbands, admits that she is secretly in love with Karna. Everyone blames her for housing such deceit in her heart. Krishna then tells everyone to eat a jambul and if there is not a single deceit in their heart, the fruit won't dye their mouth. Everyone's mouth froths in purple! The moral here is that everyone has a secret, and we must not look down upon those who do, and those who articulate it. Also, note how different Krishna is from Jamadagni who cuts off his wife's head for merely thinking about another man. Krishna is thus seen as this broad-minded figure, which is why people are so easily attracted to him, because who doesn't love a man who understands?

Tale 71

Local Stories from Kerala

Kerala has a vibrant storytelling tradition. One of its most famous folk tales is 'Parayi Petta Panthirukulam'. A regular participant of Teatime Tales pointed me towards this tale that I had no clue about. The story goes that Vararuchi, one of the Navratnas of Vikramaditya's court, is set to marry a lower-caste woman. But he does not know that she is from the lower caste, since she was raised by Brahmin parents. By the time he realizes this, it is too late. He accepts his fate. He accepts that nature, and fate, do not care for his bigotry.

The couple get married and go on a pilgrimage. During this, every time the couple has a child, Vararuchi would ask his wife, 'Does the child have a mouth?' If she answers in the affirmative, he will tell her to leave the child on the ground and move on, for someone else will come and feed the child. In this way they forsake eleven children. Each child is adopted by a loving couple, each one belonging to a different point on the spectrum of caste. It reveals the kindness of all castes and Vararuchi accepts the folly of caste ideology.

The twelfth child, however, does not have a mouth, and so Vararuchi consecrates this child on a hill in Palakkad district, which is now known as the Vayillakunnilappan Temple. This is an interesting story, because caste comes to Kerala from the Gangetic plains in the North, and Kerala retains the memory of it by becoming a very hierarchical and stratified society. In a way, this story is trying to unite the different castes by creating a common origin story.

Each adopted child, a mix of high and low caste, raised by a third caste, is a genius in his own right in the particular vocation he is obliged to follow on account of caste rules. For example, one child is a great trader, and another is a philosopher. One of these children, who is a great architect, is asked to build a pond. But the three different communities of that village ask for three different kinds of ponds—one asks for a circular one, one asks for a rectangular one, and one asks for a square one. The architect was so skilled that when he made the pond, all three communities were satisfied depending on the angle they saw the pool from—from one angle the pond looked circular, from one it was rectangular, and from one square. The pool was the same, it was only our perspective and thus our experience of it that changed.

....

Why Stop at Seventy-two?

Seventy-two is an important number across cultures. Christians believe Jesus Christ came back to life after seventy-two hours. Then, there's also one of my favourite Biblical stories about Jacob (Yakub) who leaves his house after a gruesome fight with his brother Esau. He ends up sleeping out in the open, using a rock as his pillow. In the night he dreams of a ladder with seventy-two rungs. It is said that there are some angels climbing up the rungs, while some are tumbling down, like a game of snakes and ladders. This ladder is the connection between earth and heaven. There are seventy-two steps towards infinity, and it is a difficult path—you will rise, you will fall, but the eyes must always look onward and upward.

The number seventy-two also finds mention in other religions. The Jewish Kabbalah has seventy-two names for God. In Borobudur, the largest Buddhist temple in Indonesia, there are seventy-two stupas. In Angkor Wat, of the ancient Khmer kingdom in Cambodia, there are seventy-two temples. Then, of course, there is the much discussed notion of the seventy-two Houris of Jannat. I find it fascinating that the Islamic heaven, with Houris and fountains and food, is so different from the Christian heaven which is, for all intents and purposes, non-sexual, non-sensual. Such opposition is often found in neighbouring cultures, a self-conscious distancing from the other, known to anthropologists as schismogenesis.

Seventy-two is also a perfectly divisible number. You divide it by three, you get twenty-four, and thus the twenty-four tirthankaras. You divide it by eight, you get nine, and thus the Navadwaras, or the nine gates of the body—two eyes, two ears, two nostrils, one mouth, one anus, and one of genitalia. It is such a neat number, filled with rich significance, and so I decided to stop here.

Endnote

Often during the webcast of Teatime Tales, I would lose my temper with people who would flood in with their troll-like questions, deriving pleasure from stupidity. It was during one such session that I had an epiphany—the distinction between a swan and a cockroach. While Saraswati's swan is believed to be able to separate milk from water, the cockroach looks for nourishment in the gutter. There will always be people who want to understand and those who revel in ignorance. The swan and the cockroach. Everybody has a place in society. Therefore, it is perfectly fine if people choose not to learn. The burden is not only with the transmitter. It is also with the receiver. It takes two to glean the wisdom of a tale. *The Stories We Tell* (and its progenitor, Teatime Tales) wants people to expand their minds. But if they don't, that, too, is okay.